# HART BEATS

SERENADE, #1

## DREW DUNCAN

**HART BEATS**
Copyright © 2021 Drew Duncan
All rights reserved.

No part of this book may be reproduced or transmitted in any form or
by any means, electronic or mechanical, including photocopying,
recording, or by any other information storage and retrieval system
without the written permission of the author, except in the case of brief
quotations embodied in critical articles and reviews. This book is a work
of fiction, all names, characters, places, and events are the products of
the author's imagination, or are used fictitiously. Any resemblance to
actual persons, living or dead, events, or locations is entirely
coincidental. All rights reserved. Except as permitted under the UK
Copyright, Designs and Patents Act 1988.

EDITING BY: Karen Sanders Editing
FORMATTING BY: Irish Ink Publishing
PRE-MADE COVER BY: FuriousFotog

*To the man who inspires me*

# CHAPTER 1
## ALEX

I closed the door behind him, slumped against it, and let the tears fall. I had been holding on to the emotions swarming me since I got home from our latest tour. But now it all came spilling out. I had found my boyfriend and one third of the band I was in balls deep in our manager's twenty-two-year-old daughter. Our relationship was over, our band was over. My life felt like it was over.

Trust Preston Phillips to take fucking up to a whole new level. The band was in tatters, our manager was bailing on us, and my relationship with the man I had loved since I was seventeen was over. The last nine years wiped out with one sordid little affair. I let the tears fall. I needed to let it out; my life as I knew it was over.

It wasn't the fact that he had cheated on me with a woman that hurt me the most. He was bisexual, and that had never been a secret. His ex right before me was female. It was that Preston was as indignant as ever when confronted about what the hell he was thinking by shagging the girl he had been around since she was the tender age of thirteen.

"Just because you're not as hot as that anymore, Alex," he announced. "Why would I want to dip my wick in brass when I can be banging some platinum pussy?"

He had the nerve to stand there silently, like he was waiting for me to answer him. Like I was about to turn around and tell him I agreed. What I don't think he was expecting was the answer he got.

"Well, this brass ass would like to see your plasticine prick drop off while you move your shit out of my fucking house."

His expression was priceless.

"Plasticine, Alex?"

"Sad, soft, and just makes a mess everywhere." I glared at him. "Get the fuck out, NOW! JUST... Just fuck off, Preston. We're done," I told him and walked away.

"You can't kick me out, Alex. Where will I go? We can talk about this..." He grovelled in this pathetic way that just a day before would have had me feeling sorry for him. *Not anymore.*

I rolled my eyes at his level of selfishness. Only Preston could cheat on me, ruin my life, and then have the balls to ask why I was pissed at him, and try to make me feel sorry for him. Un-fucking-believable.

I wiped my cheeks and tried to gather myself together. Preston Phillips might have knocked me on my ass, ripped out my heart, *and* destroyed our band, but he couldn't break me. He had tried, but I refused to give in completely.

My mobile rang in my pocket. 'Delaney Everett' flashed on the screen. My ex-manager. *Well, shit. What the hell would this be about now?*

"Del?" I asked.

"Listen. I know you said the band was done..."

"I did."

"And I know I went apeshit and said I wouldn't repre-sent any of you again."

"You did."

"Well... maybe I was a bit hasty with that. I mean, you were a victim in this disaster too."

Oh, Christ. Just the sound of that word made me feel sick. Is that what I was to people? A victim? Del's voice continuing made me snap out of my cringing. "I've had something come up that might work perfectly for you."

A pregnant pause hung in the air while Delaney waited for my reply.

"Go on," I prompted after a second or so.

"Well, you have, of course, heard of the other band I represent, right? Spitfire Junction?"

Of course I had heard of Spitfire Junction. They were the hottest things on the indie rock scene right then.

"I have."

"Well, their drummer has always been a bit of a flake, and the boys have collectively decided to let him go."

A lightbulb went off over my head. It was no secret that the current drummer, Andy Becker, was a coked-up disaster. He'd missed recording sessions, got in fights with roadies in the middle of live concerts, showed up for TV and radio interviews barely capable of stringing a sentence together, and had proved an embarrassment to the band's brand on more than one occasion. The man was a fucking mess, even by rock and roll standards. There was a rumour going around that, after his last bender, he was facing prison time.

"If you're asking..." I started.

"If you'll be their new drummer," Del interrupted.

"Have you spoken to the band?"

I knew Delaney well enough to know that this could very well have been one of his schemes where he got a hair-brained idea and nothing would shift it out of his head.

"They'll be fine with it," he answered.

"Have they even heard of me?" I asked, pushing him to admit this was a bad idea.

"What do you want, Alex?"

"A real audition for them. All three of the guys in the room. If they like me, well, then I'll think about joining them."

"I'll sort it," he told me and agreed to get back to me when he had organised everything before hanging up.

# CHAPTER 2

## ALEX

I walked from the goods lift into the expansive converted warehouse that was part of the studios that were about to serve as practice space for the audition I was having for Spitfire Junction.

Delaney grinned when he saw me, pulled me in, and planted a showbiz-style kiss on each cheek. "Alex, thank you so much for being here!"

I smiled politely. I felt the need to apologise for Preston's actions. "Del, I'm so sorry for everything," I started.

"Do not dare apologise for that tosser. You did nothing to me, or to Stephanie. Enough. Let's get you in to see the boys," he snapped before pointing me towards an enclosed sound stage.

I had never met Spitfire Junction, but they were all over the media, rising fast through the ranks to the dizzy heights of stardom. Nothing would have prepared me for the sight of them in the flesh.

Travis Cooper, the bass guitarist, was easily six feet two and was muscular without being bulky. His jet-black hair was shoulder length in braids. His skin was a rich chestnut colour, and his eyes were shrouded in thick lashes and were a rich sienna brown with hazel flecks that sparkled mischievously.

Johnny Scott, second guitarist, was about five feet ten, built like a tank, with long, fair poker-straight hair which he wore in a long plait down his back. His eyes were piercing green, and his pink lips against long facial hair struck me as full and utterly kissable. When he caught me looking, he gave me a little wink. I glanced away; the man was pure sex appeal, and a fella could get burned looking at such a sight.

Dexter Lovell was Spitfire Junction's lead singer and guitarist. He was in between the heights of his bandmates. His hair was short, spiked, and bright blue, matching his sparkling eyes. His grin hinted at a cheekiness that shone with sexuality. As I looked at the three men before me, I felt heat creeping over my face and spreading over my body, right down to my cock. They were beyond handsome and edgy, raw sex appeal.

*Shit. This could get dangerous.* Part of me thought about thanking them for the opportunity there and then and walking away. But I didn't get the chance.

"Boys," Del announced. "Let me introduce you to Alex Hart. He was the drummer of the recently split AP3. He knows about the issues you guys have been having with Andy. I think he'd be a great fit with the band."

Travis glared in my direction. "He's bad luck," he stated, raising a laugh from Johnny.

Dexter rolled his eyes and held out an outstretched hand. "Hi, Alex. Ignore the goon behind me. You're very welcome."

I took his hand and smiled. "Yeah. Thanks for meeting

with me." His hand was warm and soft, and he radiated energy I could feel myself being put at ease by.

Johnny stepped forward, nudged Dexter in the ribs, and grinned. "Stop hogging the limelight, bellend!" He laughed, and again, I felt the heat of a blush creeping over my skin.

"I'm Johnny, love. It's a pleasure to meet you," he said, taking my hand and placing his lips against my knuckles.

Travis groaned. "Thanks for coming, Alex, but I don't know if this is going to work."

Delaney stepped in to ease Travis's concerns. "Now, Travis. We talked about this. Alex is the best drummer around. He will work well with Spitfire Junction. I thought you trusted me," he added, almost blackmailing Travis with guilt into accepting me.

Travis grumbled. "Whatever." He sighed and turned to the amp, then started to mess with the controls like it was the most important thing in the world.

Delaney rolled his eyes and nodded towards the drum kit behind the rest of the band. "Alex, if you want to get yourself settled in there, and I'll let you and the lads get on with it." He smiled and headed back towards the door, leaving me to feel like a lamb being left to the wolves.

# CHAPTER 3
## JOHNNY

*Well, well, well!* I thought when the nervous-looking blond guy walked in with Delaney. I was very interested in him, regardless of what happened with him and the band. He was the perfect height, approximately five feet seven. He was toned without too much bulk. He was just perfectly proportioned, and the cute flash of colour that liked to creep over his face connected directly with my dick.

My eyes ran over his body, over his full lips, and my mind ran with the idea of how sweet his mouth would taste, and how good it would feel wrapped around my prick. When I looked at his face, I could see he was focused on my mouth as much as I focused on his. I smiled and gave him a little wink, taking delight in the soft blush that crept across his skin as I did. I wondered if that was how he would look if he was under me.

I was distracted from my illicit thoughts by Travis's comment about him being bad luck. A laugh snorted out of me. Travis always found it difficult to deal with change.

For such a smart man, he was always so full of superstitious nonsense about lucky this, or unlucky that.

Dexter was his usual courteous self, shaking Alex's hand and making him feel welcome after Travis's outburst. I grinned and moved towards him, nudging Dex in the ribs as I did, taking Alex's hand.

"Stop hogging the limelight, bellend." I smirked, looking him straight in the eyes to make sure he knew I wasn't unhappy to have him there. "I'm Johnny, love. It's a pleasure to meet you." I smiled and lifted his hand to my mouth. The second my lips made contact with his skin, I felt it everywhere. My cock stirred against my jeans. *This is going to get very interesting.*

Del told Alex to head over to the drum kit and get himself settled. I glanced over at Dexter, and he gave me a look that told me he knew I liked the look of our lovely potential new bandmate. Wasn't he a lucky lad? He already had Dexter ready to punch me in the balls over him.

Time to see what this guy could do behind the kit. Honestly, anything would be better than what Andy was capable of lately, but I actually wanted it to work out with Alex. It would give us back that edge, something to take away the bullshit of Andy's latest round of coked-up bullshit, even if Alex did have a little baggage from his previous bandmate and ex.

Alex got himself ready, adjusted his seat, and checked he was in the perfect spot to knock it out of the park. If he was at all nervous, it didn't really show.

"How about we start with a cover?" Dexter suggested.

"Sure. What did you have in mind?" Alex smiled.

"What about The Who? You know *My Generation,* right?" Travis asked.

*Fucker.* We all knew the song, and there were plenty of people out there who would rank it up there in the top ten hardest tracks for a drummer. I knew what he was up to. He wanted Alex to fall flat on his handsome face. I was about to speak up when Alex smirked and responded to Travis's challenge.

"Challenge accepted, big guy." He grinned, and my cock stirred against my jeans. Well, fuck. Not only was he hot, he had balls of steel and had come armed to a fist fight. "Ready?" he asked. The guys nodded, and he started a count-in. "1-2-3-4."

He kicked the song off into high gear instantly, leaving Travis and me to follow in, and Dexter tapping his foot, waiting for his cue. Within a minute of playing, I couldn't help but grin. Alex came alive behind a drum kit, and the look on Travis's face told me he knew his plan was not going to work. Alex was not going to fail, or not be just what the band needed. It didn't matter what we played after that, even some of our rarer album bonus tracks. Alex had done his homework and knew them all. He was a force to be reckoned with, and I couldn't help but feel proud of how well he handled it, even if I didn't really know him.

# CHAPTER 4
## DEXTER

WHEN DELANEY ASKED US TO TAKE A LOOK AT A NEW drummer, I'd agreed. It was something we badly needed. Andy was a liability, and I didn't think we would make it as a band if we kept him on any longer. The man couldn't see further than his next score, and like it or not, this was a business. We were lucky enough to be making money doing something we loved, but Andy was killing our brand. We were getting more fame and notoriety for his indiscretions and fuck-ups than we were for the music we were playing.

Then Delaney told me who he had in mind. I did my best not to balk at the suggestion of Alex Hart. I knew he was a great drummer, but he had just been through his own bullshit with his boyfriend, Preston, and I worried that would just bring more baggage to the band instead of helping us ditch the shit we already had.

"Dex," Del started, sensing my unspoken reservations. "I know what you're thinking, but he's a great lad, and a fucking amazing drummer. Sure, this bullshit with that wanker Phillips isn't ideal, but you have nothing to worry about with Alex. I promise you that. I wouldn't be recommending him if I didn't think he was going to be a great fit for you and the rest of the fellas." He gripped my shoulder, as if to enforce his genuine appreciation of my concerns and Alex's ability to fit in with us.

"Thanks, Del. I'm just worried about how we could look, ditching one load of drama to take on a different kind of drama. Is he definitely done with Phillips and their band?" I asked.

He nodded. "He's kicked him out, and yes, the band is most definitely over. I'm not sure anyone wants Preston Phillips around anymore."

My turn to nod. I knew Preston had been caught with his prick in the boss's daughter. Stephanie was a lovely girl; more than lovely, really, but like Alex and his band, we had all been around her since she was a young teen. The thought of seeing her as anything other than a younger sister was alien to all of us. Preston had cheated on his long-term boyfriend by shagging that same 'younger sister' and made everyone feel generally creeped out by how it all happened. That was definitely not something our brand needed to be tainted with.

I called Travis and Johnny over to my place and told them what Delaney had suggested.

"Well, Del thinks we should give him an audition," I explained.

"Why would we want him in the band?" Travis asked. "It just complicates things even more."

Johnny grinned, as usual. "I think it's a fucking great idea, mate. I mean, sure, Preston Phillips is the biggest fucking wanker I've ever come across, but Alex didn't do that, and I think it would be good for all of us to move on from our respective bad histories."

Ever the optimist was Johnathan Scott; it was one of

the things we loved and loathed in him all at the same time. It could be a breath of fresh air sometimes, and others, it could leave you wanting to kick him in the balls.

Travis sighed. "You really don't get it, do you? What if they bring their shit with them, and we end up with even more bullshit to deal with?" he asked. "Then what? He takes the band down with him like he did with AP3?"

"I'm not sure that's a fair comparison," Johnny replied.

I had to agree with my bud. I didn't think the evaporation of AP3 was something that could be dumped at Alex's door. "Travis, I get it, I really do. But I don't think the end of AP3 had much to do with Alex Hart, and a lot more to do with a certain Preston Phillips being found balls deep in the boss's kid."

Johnny's eyes rolled. "I'm a fucking creep, and even I wouldn't do that shit. There are just some lines you aren't meant to cross. That is most definitely one of them!"

"Okay, but what if ballbag here," he nodded in Johnny's direction, "gets bored one day and decides to play a game of hide the salami with our newest bandmate? And then, for whatever reason, because, let's face it, he's a fucking whore, it doesn't work out. Is that really the kind of environment any of us want to be working in?" Travis argued.

Johnny actually had the balls to grin at the implication. And I got what Travis was talking about. He had a point. Johnny wasn't the greatest boyfriend material in the world. His headboard had more notches in it than a hooker's, but was that really a valid reason for excluding someone who actually had talent, the ability to give us something different, and break into a new fanbase? It was something to think about.

"What about a pact then?" Johnny offered.

"A pact?" Travis echoed.

"Yes, a pact," Johnny repeated. "If we like him, and we take him on, we all agree right here and now that I won't cross that line and mix business and pleasure. Under no circumstances will I shit where I eat."

Travis snorted. "You really think that's a deal you can stick with, buddy?"

I smirked. Johnny was a filthy cad, and I wasn't sure his cock had ever found an arsehole it didn't like.

"I'll agree to do it for you guys," he stated.

I wiped my hand down my face. I knew this would only end in disaster, but who was I to disbelieve the guy I had been best friends with since we started school, aged four? Johnny offered his hand to us to shake on the deal. A gentleman's agreement between three friends. He would not fraternise with our potential new drummer if we decided we wanted him in the band.

"Fine. Deal," Travis grumbled, and we all shook on it.

Well, well, well. It looked like our profile was about to change.

# CHAPTER 5

## ALEX

The guys worked me hard for my audition. They threw everything they could at me, Travis especially, hoping I would slip up and give them a reason to not take me on. I played like my life depended on it, and I guess, in a way, it did. With the drama over the last few weeks, I had forgotten just how much I needed to play to feel alive. How much I needed to take my frustrations out by beating my sticks against the stretched-out skin on the top of a drum. When we finished, I was covered in sweat, my hair stuck to my face, and I was flushed from the raw energy I had put into playing.

Johnny threw a towel in my direction when we were done. "Dry yourself off there, love. You're looking a bit hot and bothered." He grinned. It was a good job I was already flushed because I'm sure my face would have been a giveaway to where my mind went with his comment.

Dexter unplugged his guitar and set it back down on the stand beside him before turning to me. "Damn, you really can play," he said, sounding genuinely surprised.

A laugh escaped me. "Would I be here if I couldn't play at the level you guys need?"

"True. I mean it, though. Some of those tracks even Andy had trouble with when he was having a good day. You're a fucking natural."

Now I did feel heat in my cheeks, proud to have someone as talented as Dexter Lovell think I had any kind of musical gift. "Thanks, Dexter."

Travis also appeared by where Dexter and Johnny were standing in front of the drum kit. He reached out his hand for me to shake. "Welcome to Spitfire Junction, Alex," he said when I took his hand in mine. The other two lads grinned in Travis's direction.

"Yes!" Johnny cheered, and Dexter laughed.

"Really?" I exclaimed in excitement.

Dexter nodded. "Works for me, Alex."

I cheered myself and jumped up from the stool, raising my arms in victory. Johnny grinned, moved round the drum set, and threw his arms around me. He laughed at his three bandmates and called out to them. "Get over here, you bitches."

Johnny's hand was around my waist, pulling me closer to him, and Travis and Dexter just shook their heads and slung their arms over each other's shoulders. Suddenly, I realised just how much I needed this. To feel like I was a part of a team again. A team that wasn't about to act in the same way Preston had.

After a moment, I attempted to break contact with the guys. Any longer in the middle of their manwich and things would have got very awkward. They were all gorgeous, but I wasn't about to let that get in the way of all the possibilities I had now. This needed to be completely professional.

———

I WAS GOING TO BE THROWN IN AT THE DEEP END. THE GUYS were due to leave on a tour in just five weeks. I needed to get myself organised to get out on the road so soon after arriving home from my own tour with AP3. There was to be a general press release issued. Andy wasn't sacked, he had decided to take time out and put himself into rehab. In the meantime, they would announce that I would be standing in for their upcoming tour.

It was going to generate an incredible amount of attention. When we weren't rehearsing, we were on the press junket; late night talk shows, radio shows, morning television magazine shows. My introduction to the world of Spitfire Junction would be a baptism of fire.

"HOT ON THE BREAK-UP OF HIS RELATIONSHIP FROM FRONT man Preston Phillips, Alex Hart is now standing in for the misfit drummer of Spitfire Junction, Andy Becker. They'll be here to tell us all about it later."

I winced when I heard Phillip Schofield explain our appearance on *This Morning* in just forty-five minutes.

Johnny caught my gaze and smiled at me. "Don't worry, love. We'll shoot that shit down for you," he reassured me, and warmth crept over me. He was protective of me, and I found it endearing. It was still a novel concept to have someone being concerned with how I was feeling about things.

Dexter agreed with Johnny. "It's all good, Alex. We've got your back." He put his hand on my shoulder to let me know he meant it.

Travis nudged my back. "If all else fails, we'll have Johnny flirt with Holly." He smiled.

Damn, the guys were amazing. It had only been two weeks since my audition, and this was our first outing on daytime TV, but already they were looking after me and looking out for me. If things were too uncomfortable for me, they deflected the questions or comments away from me and the topic the interviewer was focusing on. I already felt like I was well and truly part of their team.

———

FORTY-THREE MINUTES LATER AND WE WERE SITTING ON the sofa opposite Phillip Schofield and Holly Willoughby.

"So, Alex, how does it feel to be spending so much time with these gorgeous fellas?" Holly asked.

I smiled. "Honestly, Holly, they have me working so hard, I haven't had a chance to think about it. We've been rehearsing so much for the upcoming tour."

Holly nodded and looked at Phillip, letting him know it was his turn. "Will you be replacing Andy Becker permanently?" he asked me.

Dexter was instantly in with a reply on my behalf. "Andy is like a brother to us. It's not that he could just be replaced, but he has some problems he needs to give his full attention to. He needs to get healthy, and at the minute, being in the band isn't providing him with the stability he needs. So, Alex graciously agreed to help us out with that."

I smiled, listening to Dexter's diplomatic reply. They weren't saying they had 100% ousted Andy, but they also weren't saying I wasn't a permanent replacement.

"So, the upcoming tour. It's sold out everywhere. How are you handling that level of interest?" Holly asked.

Johnny stepped in this time. "Well, I think I can speak for everyone here when I say we are all incredibly flattered by the response of the public to the band, and it's very humbling to know we're being so well received. What about you, Holly?" Johnny said with a wink. "What's your personal favourite of our tracks?"

And there it was, Johnny flirting with Holly Willoughby, live on *This Morning*. Travis looked at me and smirked. She blushed, thought about it, gave her answer, and Phillip only had enough time to tell us good luck with the tour. Just like that, the interview was done. "The guys will be back after the break to play us out with their latest hit," he announced.

———

"You were amazing!" Dexter smiled at me when everything was over.

"Oh, I dunno about that." Johnny sulked. "He said he hadn't noticed how hot we all are!"

Travis groaned. "Thinking with the wrong head again, Johnny?" He glared. Johnny laughed, but dropped it and walked away.

I felt like I was missing something. I knew Johnny was a philanderer and a flirt. Was there something about me and my brass ass that meant he couldn't be that way with me?

# CHAPTER 6

### JOHNNY

*FOUR WEEKS LATER*

THE SIGHT OF HIM STRUGGLING WITH HIS CASE AND DRUM bags towards the tour bus had me rushing over to assist him.

"Hey. Need a hand with that?" I asked him. He smiled and blew a stray hair out of his face. I couldn't help myself; I reached forward and moved the hairs out of his eyes, touching his cheek as I did and feeling my stomach flip. *Shit.* I quickly looked away and grabbed his case from his hand. "Your carriage awaits, love." I grinned and motioned towards the bus parked up in the yard of the studios.

He laughed, and it was a sound that rang in my ears. It was sweet and appealing, and I shook my head to stop the thoughts that were starting to swim around, wondering how to get that laugh out of him more, how to get him to make other sounds, and just how sexy and adorable those might sound. I pulled his case to Jimmy, who was busy loading everything under the bus for us. This was the nice thing about being on tour now we were the next hot thing. We had more space than we had when we were starting out. The bus was exclusively for us and our shit. Everything else was in a truck that followed us. Aside from our cases and the odd acoustic guitar, everything else had a different way of getting there. It made a refreshing change from moving to and from gigs in the back of Dexter's Ford Transit, an amp slamming into the back of my seat when Dexter applied the brakes a little too hard sometimes.

Once I had Alex's case taken care of, I ushered towards the main door. "M'lord," I said, bowing before him. He laughed again and started up the steps of the coach. My eyes couldn't help but fall on his rounded arse, and my body reacted to what I was looking at. *Double shit!* I followed him up the stairs, only to be met with a grinning Dexter at the top step.

"Like what you see there, buddy?" He smirked at me. *Busted. Fuck.*

I glared at him and muttered a stern "Fuck off" as I passed him. I growled at myself.

Nope, that wasn't going to happen. I might be famed man whore Johnny Scott, but even I could fucking control myself. But then I looked again at Alex, catching another glimpse of his arse as my eyes betrayed me, and I really wasn't so sure this was something I would be able to avoid.

———

I HEADED TO THE BACK OF THE BUS AND SETTLED MYSELF into the corner, as far as the confines of our transport would allow me. I needed to steel myself. I knew I wouldn't be able to dodge him forever. He was tough, and sassy, and yet there was a certain element of vulnerability about him that made me want to protect him.

Dexter sank into the seat opposite me. "You're staring, mate."

Fuck. I hadn't even realised I had been looking at him all that time.

"Don't know what you're talking about," I murmured and turned my gaze out the window instead.

Dexter laughed. "You can't kid a kidder. But you made a deal, remember?"

"I know," I snapped back at him.

He held his hand up in defeat. "I get it, big guy. Honestly, I do, but we can't afford to have this blow up in our faces, and you promised."

I looked at him incredulously. "I've found a fella I don't want to sink my cock into. Okay!"

Dexter rolled his eyes. "I'm not dead, John. I understand that we *all* have needs. But we've had enough shit around our band's name, and so has he. So, I hope for your sake the lie you're telling yourself turns out to be true."

It was the one thing I admired most about Dexter. He was blunt, and honest, and didn't pull any shit. I also had to agree with him. While, yes, Alex was a sexy man who any man would be lucky to get the chance to satisfy, that wasn't all there was to him. Lust wasn't the only thing he inspired in me, apparently. But we had worked too long and too hard on the band and getting where we were to throw it all away.

"Honest, boss. I will not stick my dick in the hot little drummer boy." I laughed.

Dexter groaned, and with that, the spell was broken. He gave me the disgust I needed to shake off the feelings that were rising about Alex. "Classy as always, Johnathan.

Classy as always. Now, fuck off. I'm going to get some kip."
He kicked my foot.

I laughed again and lifted myself from the chair. "Fine.
I know when to take a hint." I smirked and moved off to
set myself down in front of Alex instead.

# CHAPTER 7

## ALEX

I watched the interaction of my bandmates, Johnny and Dexter, having a secret hushed conversation in the back corner of the bus, all the while making occasional glances in my direction. They weren't very subtle. It was pretty damn obvious that I was the topic of conversation, and for the first time, I felt uneasy around them. I was filled with dread that I was stuck on a tour with a couple of guys who might not actually have wanted me there. I could hear Preston's voice in my head, pointing out a million and one reasons I wasn't good enough to be there. My faults, my flaws, the things that made me a misfit everywhere. He preferred brunettes; I was blond. He preferred tall fellas and short women; I was five seven. He preferred slim girls with tits that could fit in his hand and slim fellas with very little muscles. While I wasn't fat, I had been well-blessed in the muscle department and was toned and thicker than he liked. All of this reinforced further by finding him in bed with Del's daughter. A petite, thin, brunette, with a modest cleavage, and worst of all, younger. Everything I could never be.

I watched them from the corner of my eye as Johnny got up. I pretended I had been finding something out the window very interesting instead of noticing the looks and whispers. He plonked himself into the chair next to me.

"Hello, love. Are you all set for your first exciting adventure as part of Spitfire Junction?" he asked.

I sighed. "Am I part of Spitfire Junction, Johnny?" I hadn't meant to be so blunt, but the words just fell out of my mouth. I couldn't hold my insecurity in.

Johnny stared at me. "Why the hell wouldn't you be? You're here, aren't you?" He gestured around the tour bus.

"What was all that about then?" I said, nodding towards where Dexter was now sitting alone, his arms folded over his chest and his eyes closed.

For a split second, Johnny winced, and my heart sank. I had definitely caught him out in something. "That wasn't what you think, sweetness. Trust me, you don't even want to know what that was about."

I glared. I honestly thought things had settled, and that it had been agreed that I was a good fit for the band. I guess he was just a very good actor.

Johnny seemed to read my face. "Alex, listen," he started. "That wasn't about anyone not wanting you here. It was about him giving me shit for being flirty. You know me. I'm a bit of a tease, and God knows I'll sink my cock into almost any sweet piece of ass that crosses my path. Dexter just wants to make sure I'm on the same page as the rest of the guys. That you're a great fit for the Spitfires and I can't allow my libido to fuck that up for us."

My face flushed. So, I *was* the kind of fella Johnny would be interested in normally? When I realised that was the first place my mind went instead of being relieved that it wasn't about me not fitting into the band, I blushed more.

Johnny put his hand on my knee. "Are you okay? I'm sorry, love. I didn't want you to think that it was something like you not fitting in. I just needed to be honest and tell you where my mind was, and that Dexter was trying to drum sense into me."

I glanced down at his hand, his thumb rubbing circles on the inside of my knee, and I felt the contact sizzling right up my thigh and into my dick. Johnny's eyes followed mine, realised what he was doing, and pulled his hand back.

"Shit, I'm sorry. See, this is what Dexter means. I'm such a tart. I don't even realise I'm doing it. It's just second nature." He held both hands in the air. "I promise I will not hit on you. I mean it."

Johnny's smile was warm, and I should have felt reassured by it. Instead, I just felt a faint sting of rejection. I got the logic behind it. Hell, I agreed with it 100%. I wanted to fit in with the band. I loved being a part of it. I wanted to stay, and I didn't need something to mess that up and make the whole thing uncomfortable. But with everything that had happened of late, all I felt was unwanted. Damn Preston Phillips and what he was still doing to me. I guess I had been more under his spell and put upon more than I ever realised.

I forced a smile at Johnny and changed the subject to the tour. I knew the list of dates and some of the itinerary, but I needed to talk about some of it. We were on our way from London to Edinburgh. We had a show there the following night, then we played Newcastle, then Manchester, Liverpool, Birmingham, Cardiff, Bristol, Portsmouth, and then London for the grand finale. Plans were already being worked on for a big European tour to follow.

Johnny answered everything I asked and ran down the

standard practice for each stop. Travel by bus, arrive at a nice hotel, stay there, play some music for people, then back on the bus to the next stop of the tour. Apparently, in most places, we would take over a whole floor, a bedroom each, traditionally one room after the other, with Del usually staying on the same floor with us. I nodded, digesting everything I was told.

Travis boarded and came to where Johnny and I were sitting and took the seat right beside me. He nudged me and grinned. "Well, are you ready for the heady adoration of Spitfire Junction's screaming fans?"

I laughed. When I was alone, I had taken a quick look on Twitter to see what the response was like to me joining the band. Most of the tweets were very supportive of me and the boys. They were sorry to hear about Andy's problems and glad he was getting help. They thought I was a great drummer and would be fab in the band in Andy's absence. Hell, even a few had said how I shouldn't be his stand-in, I should just join the band and that should be that. But then there were the die-hard fans who were so much in adoration of the band that it was almost delusional. I was a fuck-up and a mess. How dare I get involved with *their* boys? There had even been a few comments about Preston being right to trade me in and cheat, and how they would have too.

"I'm not sure everyone thinks of it that way." I smiled.

Johnny glared. "You've been on Twitter, haven't you?" Damn, this man was too fucking good at reading me.

"Maybe," I admitted guiltily.

Travis laughed. "Jesus, Alex. Are you a glutton for punishment? Why would you torture yourself like that? I mean, I love our fans, but fucking hell, have you read what they say on social media? Some of them need some serious psychiatric help!"

Johnny burst out in a hearty belly laugh. "Christ, do you remember that one in Seattle? She'd been messaging the page on Facebook every day for two months beforehand, and then when we didn't recognise her at the concert, she had a total meltdown?"

Travis looked at my horrified expression. "No, no. She didn't actually meet us. She was on the balcony, about 100 metres back from the stage, and she got so pissed that we hadn't spotted her and acknowledged that she was there."

My horror changed to shock. How the hell did they deal with this level of dedication and adoration from fans? I mean, AP3 had their hardcore supporters, but nothing that went to that level.

"You're in the big leagues now, Alex. You'll have to get used to the utter insanity of some people who buy our records." Johnny laughed.

I shook my head. "Guys, I'm not sure I could ever get used to that level of crazy."

Travis looked at me sincerely, and I felt my fears ease. His hand found its way to my shoulder. "Well, you're not going anywhere. You're one of us now. So, you had just better get used to it." He squeezed my shoulder. I felt Johnny's eyes taking in what Travis was doing. A slight eyebrow raise graced his features, and then it disappeared. Travis pulled his hand back, and I smiled, admitting I would have to give it a go and thanking him for making me feel so welcome.

# CHAPTER 8

## ALEX

*Just to let you know, I've moved back into the house while you're on tour. I didn't think you'd mind xx*

I stared at my phone in complete disbelief. He honestly thought he could move into my house again after everything he'd done and I would be okay about it? Preston's level of insanity in the aftermath of our break-up was borderline psychotic.

I could feel Johnny's eyes on me. "What's wrong?" he asked.

I pursed my lips and hammered out an angry reply to Preston. "My fucking ex has moved back into my house while we're on tour."

*What the fuck do you mean you've moved back into MY house Preston?!? You have no right, even if I'm not fucking there!!*

I hit send and locked the phone again, looking up at Johnny.

"Not too bright that fucker, is he, love?" Johnny asked. "I mean, first he gives you up, and now he's doing his best to piss you off."

"Yeah. Pissing me off is something he's incredibly good at."

Just then, Dexter stood up and announced that we had arrived at The Caledonia, Edinburgh's Waldorf Astoria. Right then, all I needed to do was find the bar. I was the first up and out of my seat. I was ready to get off and get my shit into my room then find the bar and stay there. My blood was boiling. How fucking dare Preston think he would be welcome to just camp out in my house when I wasn't there? Least of all because it was MY house. I owned it lock, stock and barrel, and most of all, because we had broken up. The lying, cheating bastard had some fucking big brass balls, I'd give him that.

Johnny followed me closely as I stormed into the hotel. "Alex. Wait up!" he called after me. I paused and allowed him to draw level with me. "Are you going to be okay?" he asked softly.

I nodded. "I just need to check in and find the bar." I sighed, feeling my phone vibrate in my hip pocket.

*I don't know why you need to be like this after everything. I mean I thought you would appreciate me keeping the house safe for you.*

I fumed at the screen. He really had lost his ever-loving mind. Johnny took one look at me and took a step back. I hit call instead of send message and waited for Preston to answer. He picked up after a few rings.

"What the actual fuck is wrong with you?" I seethed down the phone.

He actually had the cheek to laugh at me. "Lovely to hear from you too, Alex."

"Preston, I'm calling my brother. If you are not out of my house by the time he gets there, I'm calling the fucking police and having you arrested for breaking and entering and trespassing. Am I making myself clear enough for you, you utter dickhead?"

"Now, there's no need for name-calling, Alex."

"Get. The. Fuck. Out. Of. My. House!" I raged through gritted teeth and hung up the phone. I quickly dialled my brother's number. "Nicky, that fucker is in my house. Can you go over there?" I pleaded.

"Are you serious?" Nick questioned. "Have you made it to Edinburgh yet?"

"I just arrived. I can't deal with this shit. I told him I was sending you over, and if he was still there, you'd be phoning the police."

"I'm on it, kid. I'll be round at yours in the next ten minutes, and if he's still there, I'll take care of him for you. Don't worry about it. I got this," Nick told me, trying to lend what support he could from so far away.

"Love you, Nicky." I smiled down the phone.

"Back at you, little bro," he said, his smile evident in his voice.

When I looked up, I could see Johnny still watching my every move. "Did you get everything sorted?" he enquired cautiously.

"As best as it can be. My older brother is going to head over to my house now and deal with him for me."

Johnny smiled and moved back towards me. "Look, the bar is right over there." He pointed. "I'll make sure you're all checked in and I'll get back to you with your room key once it's all sorted, okay? You go and get yourself a drink and calm down. Let your brother deal with your cunt ex."

I smiled back at him. "Thanks, Johnny. I really appreciate that." Johnny winked at me and went back towards the bus, and I turned and headed straight for the bar.

# CHAPTER 9
## JOHNNY

It wasn't the time for such thoughts, but damn, he was sexy when he was angry. I couldn't lie, though; his ex was really starting to get on my nerves. When I spoke to Alex, there were times when there were some very obvious traces of his ex's put-downs, and him just not feeling like the amazing human being he seemed to be. I headed back out to the bus to grab his bags for him and help him out.

"Is he okay?" Travis asked, coming over to help me lift some of the bags from under the coach.

"His ex needs someone to teach him some fucking manners," I told him. "But he's handling it for now. He's in the bar, forgetting his worries."

Travis nodded. "I've noticed how he talks about himself, and that bellend Preston better hope I never meet him, because I'll have great pleasure in telling him just what I think of him!"

"Easy tiger." I smirked. "He's got her brother going to deal with him. He only moved back into Alex's house after he left for the tour."

"Is there something wrong with him?" Dexter asked

from over my shoulder.

"Fucking sounds like it," Travis replied.

I grabbed his bag and looked at my bandmates. "Well, if he comes near him, he'll have us, won't he? Manners in how to deal with a partner will be his first lesson." Dex and Travis agreed, and I carried our bags into the hotel.

I stood beside Del at reception and smiled. "I've got your room key, and Alex's. Where is he?"

I gestured to the bar. "Ex trouble," I informed him. "Hand his key over. I said I would get his bags into his room for him."

Del glared. "That man is a menace." He handed over his room key card and mine. "Can you be trusted with this, Johnny? No shenanigans?"

I feigned being offended. "Delaney, what are you trying to say about me? Seriously, Del. He's a bandmate, and he's off limits. I couldn't even if I wanted to."

Del eyed me suspiciously. I just nodded and walked towards the lift to find our rooms.

———

I ARRIVED ON THE FLOOR WE HAD TAKEN OVER IN THE hotel and glanced down at the two key cards in my hand. Alex's room just happened to be right beside mine. *Shit.*

I put Alex's card into the reader and opened the door. I dumped his bag on the bed, pulled the curtains, turned on the small bedside lamps instead of the large overhead lights, and gave thought to opening his case and unpacking for him. But the thought of rummaging through his underwear struck me as a step over the line.

I rubbed my hand over my crotch. I really needed to get such thoughts of him out of my head or there would be no way I could resist him some time in the future. Once I was sure his room was as ready for him as it could be, I lifted the card from the slot on the wall and left for my room next door.

I repeated my routine in my room too, adjusted the lights, pulled the curtains, and unpacked my own bag. I was feeling grubby from the trip up, and I figured I would have a shower before heading downstairs to the bar, grabbing some food, and letting Alex know where he could find his room.

I let the hot spray rain down on me as I stood there, my head swimming with thoughts of how much I was attracted to Alex, how much I wanted to protect him, and show him what a fool his ex was. My hard cock throbbed as it jutted out from my body. I knew it was a mistake to give in to such thoughts, even for this, but I talked myself in to how it wasn't that bad since he wasn't really there.

I grabbed my prick in my hand and let the shower gel make my movements more slippery. I thought about Alex's smile. I thought about the curve of his arse, and the contours of his muscular shoulders and arms. I thought about his laugh and pumped myself faster, wishing I could see more of him. Wishing I could find myself between his thighs.

"FUUUCKK!" echoed around the bathroom as my cum erupted from my cock in a jet. I let go, placed both arms on the wall in front of me, closed my eyes, and let my heart rate settle back down. In my head, Alex smiled at me, and I felt a blush cross my face.

Sweet Christ, what was I, a fourteen-year-old girl? Blushing because I'd been thinking about my crush. That was just enough to snap me out of my daydream and bring me back to my senses.

I finished my shower, dried my hair off a bit, dressed, and headed down to the bar to find him.

# CHAPTER 10
## JOHNNY

About an hour and a half had passed by the time I got down to the bar and found him. Man, that lad could drink. He was on his third shot of tequila when I arrived, but apparently, he'd started with a beer and whiskey chaser, then his first shot, then another whiskey, and now he was back on the tequila.

"Hello, you," I greeted him when the bartender had finished telling me how much he'd had.

"Johnny!" He grinned at me. Damn, even drunk he was kinda sexy. "Come… come and sit here, beside…" He attempted to tap on the empty bar stool beside him and missed, pausing to concentrate harder on making his target next time. "Sit beside me," he finished when his hand finally connected with the leather.

"Alex, you are wasted." I grinned when I got into the seat beside him. "Did you eat first?"

He turned to face me. "Nope, just went straight to the alcohol," he admitted, draping himself over my shoulder. "Are you going to join me?" His booze-fume breath wafted over me as he put his hand on my shoulder.

I laughed. "On one condition, love. We eat something first."

Alex rolled his eyes, sighed, and moved himself off my shoulder. I smiled at him, but I instantly also felt a pang of regret at the loss of his closeness to my body.

I waved at the guy behind the bar and asked him for the pizza, onion rings, and fries from their limited menu. The Caley Bar was all about the many varieties of whiskey that Scotland had to offer, not the bar snacks.

"Okay, so food is ordered. Now, let's drink!" He grinned at me again, pushing a shot glass in my direction. I downed the shot in one and let the tequila burn me as it sank into my stomach, reminding myself I made a deal, and gentlemen did not take advantage of the drunk man they picked up at the bar.

He downed his own shot and looked at me. I knew that look on his face. I had seen it in men's eyes endless times, right after I told them I wouldn't be seeing them again. Johnny Scott didn't double dip, not when there was so much other ass in the world still undiscovered.

"Do you know what he called me?" he said as she started poking his finger into my bicep to punctuate his sentence. "He said I was brass, and why did he need that when she was some platinum pussy!" His finger kept poking, and my arm tensed, but that had more to do with the fist I wanted to ram down Preston Phillips' throat than the 'assault' from my hurt bandmate.

"He's a wanker, Alex," I replied. "Don't give him a second thought. He's not worth it!"

"Do you think I have a brass ass?" he asked, his eyes turning suddenly softer, pleading for me to confirm or deny his worst fears that he wasn't enough. *Damn.* He was gorgeous. His arse was solid gold as far as I was concerned, and I hadn't even sampled it yet.

*Yet?*

"I think his head is made of brass and echoes from being empty for cheating on someone like you," I replied honestly.

He smiled, and his hand hit my shoulder again. "Aww, Johnny. You're the best!" he slurred, grinning at me, leaning in, probably to keep himself upright more than anything. But for the briefest of moments, I revelled in his attention. I patted my large hand over his and gave in to a moment of temptation, kissing the top of his hand.

Drunken doe eyes looked up at me when I did, and I felt that pull towards him. I looked at his lips, plump and begging to be kissed; all I needed to do was lean forward, but I was saved by the food arriving. The barman set the pizza and other delights out, and I was forced to look away. *Shitting hell.*

We ate, and he seemed to sober up a little as the food started to soak up the bellyful of alcohol he'd had. He would still probably have a killer headache in the morning. But at least it wouldn't be as bad as it could have been.

"You have a bit of ketchup on your face," he said, waggling his finger vaguely in my direction.

I wiped my hand down my cheek. "Did I get it?"

"No." He laughed. "It's still there." He waggled his finger at my face again.

I wiped over my chin. "Better now?"

He sighed and lifted his hand to my face. His fingertip traced over my bottom lip. Without thinking, I grabbed his wrist, stuck his ketchup-covered finger in my mouth, and licked it clean.

*Big mistake, Johnny.*

My cock stirred in my jeans, and all I could think about was him and the things I wanted to do to him in a much more intimate setting.

He saw that look in my eyes and blushed, pulled his finger from between my lips, and excused himself, stumbling as he got off his stool, and headed straight for the men's restroom.

When he appeared about fifteen minutes later, his face was flushed, and he looked a bit pissed off. "You okay?" I asked.

"Nick phoned. That wanker was still in my house, strutting around in his underpants. He had to call the police, and that fucking moron punched him!"

"He smacked your brother?" I clarified.

"That motherfucker sucker-punched my brother when the cops came!"

"Tell me he was arrested!"

"Oh, yes! Arrested and taken the fuck out of my house!" Alex grinned. "It's your round, Johnny. This needs a celebration!"

I smirked, called over the barman, and ordered more whiskey.

———

THREE WHISKEYS LATER, BOTH ALEX AND I WERE FEELING the effects of the alcohol, food or no food.

"I think we need another!" Alex announced.

"I think we need to go to bed."

"Yours or mine?" He grinned at me.

"Oh, you tempting little flirt!" I grinned back. "You in yours and me in mine. Before I get too pissed to fight you off."

He looked at me with almost hurt. "You would fight me off?" he asked, rejection in his eyes and a pained look on his face.

"You're our drummer. Gorgeous and fuckable or not, I would have to," I answered candidly.

"You think I'm gorgeous and fuckable?" he asked in surprise.

Too late, I realised my mistake. Fuck it, he needed to know, my drunken mind reasoned. It wouldn't do any harm to give his confidence a boost after everything Preston had told him.

"You are the most beautiful creature I've ever seen. Don't ever forget that, no matter what your asshole ex said." I smiled at him. He sat back against the back of his stool and grinned, letting everything I said wash over him. "Now, come on. We have an early rehearsal in the morning, and I have a feeling it's not going to be fun on the amount of booze we've had."

I hopped off my stool, wobbled for a moment, and when I was sure the room was a little steadier, I held out my arm to him. "May I escort you to your room, m'lord?" I asked.

He chuckled, put his arm in mine, and stumbled as his feet dropped to the floor.

"Lead on, good sir!" He leaned heavily on my arm as we headed for the lift, and he grinned happily at whatever thought he had in his gorgeous head.

"Have you ever had sex in a lift?" he asked as we were halfway to our floor.

"Have you?"

"Ah! Ah! Ah! I asked you first." He stumbled and poked me in the chest. Instinctively, my arms reached out and grabbed him.

"No," I said softly, feeling how his body was melting into mine. It's a good thing he was drunk because he would have been able to feel how hard my cock was for him behind my jeans. Fortunately for me, he wasn't paying attention. Again, I wanted to breech that small distance between us and connect our mouths, but in the time it took me to consider the consequences, the moment was ruined by the opening of the lift door.

We stumbled out together and headed down the corridor towards the rooms. Alex's was first, then mine. We stopped by Alex's door and he fumbled with the key card, not managing to get the lock to release.

I covered his hand with mine and took the card from him. He grinned at me and moved out of the way, resting his back against the wall just beside his room door. I put the key in the slot, pulled it free, and opened the door as the green light flashed on the panel. I opened the door for him and went in to put the key card in the slot on the wall to make sure he had lights.

Stumbling drunk or not, he moved fast, and when I turned to see that he was okay, he pounced, his arms around my neck. He jumped to hook his legs around me and crushed his lips against mine. Jesus fucking Christ, his mouth was amazing. Instinct took over me, and my hands went to his arse to keep him wrapped around me. I returned his kiss, deepening it with more passion and intensity than I'd ever felt in a kiss in my life.

I allowed myself those few moments of utter bliss until he started to grind his hips against mine, and I could feel his cock hard against me. It was like slapping me in the face and bringing reality crashing down on me. I was kissing my bandmate. I was breaking my deal with my friends, my brothers, and worse still, I was taking advantage of a drunk and vulnerable man who had been through the wringer. I was a fucking douchebag.

I moved him to set him back down on the floor. He looked up at me with that same almost hurt look.

"Oh, Alex. I want you needing me like this when

you're stone-cold sober, not trying to get over your ex, and not in my band," I reasoned.

"Shit." He realised what I was getting at. "I'm sorry. I shouldn't have…" I couldn't let him finish that. I leaned in and seized his mouth with mine again, kissing him tenderly.

"Don't ever apologise for being an amazing man I can't resist." I smiled. "But I really should go."

"I know." He nodded, giving me a glum smile.

I turned without saying anything else and left. When I got safely inside my room, I punched the wall. I was crazy about him. I was utterly fucked.

# CHAPTER 11
## ALEX

I FELT LIKE THE WORST DEATH METAL THRASH BAND WAS playing in my head, my mouth felt like the Sahara, and I was in bed in yesterday's clothes. I went to sit up and the room spun too much, so I decided that lying the fuck down was the best way forward.

*Jesus Christ, what did I do last night?* I remembered being very pissed off at cuntface himself, Preston. I remembered I went to the bar. Johnny had been a sweetheart about it all. *Johnny?* I lay there, thinking about what had happened the night before. I had vague snippets of memory. I remembered the rage I had; Preston had hit my brother! I picked up the phone and sent him a text to make sure he was okay.

I remembered Johnny had offered to check me in while I went to the bar and drowned my sorrows. I remembered pizza and fries and wiping ketchup from his perfect mouth. *His mouth around my fingers.* Oh, sweet Jesus, I kissed him. I kissed Johnny Scott, and what's more, he kissed me back. I pulled the pillow over my head and cursed myself. The kiss was fucking amazing. His lips had been soft yet powerful, his tongue probing, and, God, it felt like I'd never felt in… well, ever. But he was my fucking bandmate. I was attempting to mix business with pleasure. I was fucking stupid.

I tentatively rose from the bed a second time, wondering if a shower would be enough to wash away my shame. Not shame at kissing him. Fuck, that was perfection, but the shame of knowing I wouldn't be able to repeat it. The shame of knowing I had come so close already to screwing up something amazing in my life.

Yip, not even a shower would sort that shit out, but at least I could pretend to try.

———

I STEPPED OUT OF THE LIFT AND GLANCED AROUND THE hotel lobby. None of the lads were in sight yet. Part of me was a little disappointed that Johnny wasn't around, but most of me was delighted I would be avoiding the embarrassment for a little while longer.

I turned to my right, and my eyes fell instantly on him. Johnny. I stood taking in all his glorious splendour. My eyes raked over his frame. My eyes feasted, and my body responded. Shit. This wasn't going to be the cakewalk I had fooled myself into thinking it would be. I was so attracted to Johnny that it was going to drive me insane.

He glanced over his shoulder at me walking towards him, and his eyes darkened, with the cheekiest glint to them. I felt undressed with just that one look, and my cock stiffened.

"Hey," I murmured when I arrived beside him.

He pulled me against him. "Morning, Alex. How's the head?"

I blushed at how willingly my body melded against his

without me even thinking about it. "I'm feeling a little bit fragile, to be honest." I smiled. Johnny grinned back. "Listen, about last night. I..."

Johnny's hand gripped my arse and stopped me talking as he pulled me tighter to him again. "We're good. Chill." His lips hit my forehead, and he dipped his mouth to my ear. "Some other lifetime, and you would be walking like John Wayne this morning. Now, the others are here, so behave yourself." He winked, and his hand slipped from my arse.

Travis arrived first, and from the dark look on his face, I'm pretty sure he'd noticed Johnny's movements against me. His thunderous look was zoned in on me, and the moment of lust and excitement I had felt with Johnny was lost in a heartbeat. I felt like Travis could tell everything that had happened last night and was looking at me like a disappointed parent.

"Ready to get going?" he asked, glaring at Johnny.

"Don't growl." Johnny laughed. "Alex is feeling a little delicate this morning. Too much of the great Scottish fire water last night."

I glared at him. "Thanks, Johnny. Tell everyone I can't hold my whiskey."

Dexter appeared beside Travis as I rolled my eyes at Johnny. He held out his hand to me, giving me something, and I held mine under his. He dropped three tablets into my hand; two round ones, and one capsule. "You'll need these, little drummer boy, if you want to survive today." He grinned, slapped Travis on the shoulder, and told us all to get moving.

I pulled the bottle of water from my bag, popped the pills in my mouth, and took a long drink of the cool liquid, then headed out to the bus.

# CHAPTER 12
## DEXTER

I watched them all interacting before I walked over and distracted them. I knew the look on Johnny's face, and yet there was something different about it too. He liked Alex, but there was something more to it than that. There was a gallon of lust in the look he poured over him, with his hand on his arse, but there was something deeper within it too. I saw the genuine affection in his kiss on his forehead.

Travis's small smirk faded when he saw Johnny wrapped around him, and he had to have noticed how well his body seemed to melt against his. There was certainly something between them. If I had to put money on it, I would say that they had come close to something happening between them, but as to how close, I wasn't actually sure.

*Interesting. Very interesting.* I wasn't the only one who had noticed what was apparently happening with Johnny and our new bandmate. I watched Johnny's face drop when he realised Travis's thunderous look meant that he knew something had occurred. I saw guilt on his features. Alex read his disappointment, and it saddened him. There was something lost in that look too.

Well, damn. If I didn't already know our little drummer boy had had a shit time with his ex, the look on his face now only proved it.

I was a people watcher, and as much as I was finding the little scene in front of me fascinating, it was time to kill the tension. I walked over to the group of three, held out my hand to Alex to hand him the tablets I brought for him, and patted Travis on the shoulder to encourage him to shake his foul mood.

———

WHEN WE ARRIVED AT THE EDINBURGH PLAYHOUSE, THE impending awkwardness had lifted. We had all listened in when Alex's brother had called him to let him know the latest about the pathetic display Preston had put on in his house the day before, and the sucker punch he had landed on him.

Travis's fist clenched when Alex's anger rose, and Johnny's body stiffened. My band brothers were ready to pounce for our new drummer's honour. I had to admit, there was something in me that wanted to come to his rescue just as much. He was a lovely guy who didn't deserve to feel the way he did about himself. He had fitted in with us all so damn well. Preston was a grade A asshole, and he needed to learn a lesson; the thought of schooling him appealed to me a little more than it should have. Mutual hatred of that twat seemed to make us all a little more comfortable with each other, and a little more settled into the work we had ahead of us.

We rehearsed late into the afternoon, then went back to the hotel for a little chill-out time before heading back to the Playhouse for our first sell-out gig with Alex as our drummer.

———

I GLANCED OVER MY SHOULDER AT THE END OF THE FIRST set and saw Alex was in full flow. His face was lit up, sweat beaded on his skin, and he was thoroughly enjoying himself. The crowd was hyping up the atmosphere, and the adrenaline was coursing through all of us. Everything was perfection.

At the end of the second set, we drew the song out and allowed each of us to showcase ourselves. I took great pleasure in introducing Alex to the crowd. The crowd roared their approval of him, and all three of his bandmates stood looking at him with pride. He glanced in my direction with a big grin, and I couldn't help but notice that, when his eyes made it over to Johnny, he gave him a cheeky wink. I was going to have to watch those two. There was more than just a little mutual appreciation between them, and I didn't want it to cause any issues with the band. I liked Alex. I didn't want to have to replace yet another drummer because Johnny just couldn't keep it in his pants.

# CHAPTER 13

## JOHNNY

Every venue we played at, the crowd just lapped up the fact that Alex was with us. We had played nine gigs in the last twenty days, and now we had just played to a sell-out crowd in Sheffield's City Hall.

We had all been getting along nicely, and I'll admit, despite my initial lust, I was settling into a pattern of flirty yet platonic banter with Alex. Yes, he was gorgeous. I liked him even more than I originally thought possible, but that didn't seem to matter to me. He belonged in the band; he belonged with all of us. It was just where he was meant to be, and I wasn't about to mess that up for him or us.

The venue wasn't that far from our hotel, the Leopold, so we all walked the couple of hundred yards, being stopped a few times for autographs and selfies with fans. Dex and Travis walked on ahead, and Alex and I were bringing up the rear.

Someone stopped Alex for a selfie and some drumming tips, and I let myself get a little farther ahead. The guys had already made it into the hotel when I heard the immortal words from a fan behind me. "Oh my God! It's

Preston Phillips!" I spun on my heels and looked back at Alex to find him face to face with his hideous ex.

I felt my blood boil as he touched him, holding on to him by his upper arm.

"Let go of me!" he snapped and tried to yank his arm from Preston's grip.

"I just want to talk to you, Alex," he said, attempting to sound reasonable. His grip on Alex didn't loosen.

I was on him in a second, my hand on his shoulder. "I do believe you were politely told to fuck off," I growled in his face.

He let go of Alex's arm in shock. He turned to me, squaring up to me like a lunatic. "I will thank you not to interfere when I'm talking to *my* boyfriend, mate."

"Your boyfriend? I'm your fucking ex, you nutcase. What the hell do you even want, Preston? You're a bad smell that I just can't get rid of," Alex shouted at him.

I glanced around us and noticed we were starting to draw attention, including that of one of our roadies, who just happened to follow along behind us to make sure everything was okay. I grabbed Preston by the arm and pushed him through the arches between the hotel and Wagamama and into the courtyard behind.

Big Jim, the roadie, intervened between us and the people trying to follow us and watch what was going on.

"Phillips, what the actual fuck is your problem?" I snarled at him. "We all know what you did. Why are you even here? Alex has made it clear on a few occasions now that he doesn't want you around, and yet here you are like a fucking stalker!"

"I'm just trying to make Alex understand it from my point of view," he whined.

"Your point of view?" I scoffed. "You stuck your tiny prick in a girl you had been around since she was thirteen like some fucking creepy grooming paedo, or was there something about that we all got wrong?"

Preston turned a funny shade of red, and I knew I had him. His temper was flaring, and if he really thought he was in any position to take me on, he was about to find out just how wrong he was.

"Johnny," Alex pleaded. He knew that look on Preston's pathetic face too, and it made me wonder just how many times he had seen that look before, and if he had ever turned that temper on him.

"Fuck off, Jimmy, and let me talk to my man," he spat, making a grab for Alex's arm again.

This time, I grabbed him. "It's Johnny, like you don't fucking know, and you have about four seconds to get the fuck out of here. Got it?" I snarled at him. He swung at me, and I almost ducked back out of his way, but not quite, and his pinkie ring caught me on the cheekbone. I pulled back my right hand and swung, smacking him square in the nose with a sickening crack.

"Ahhh!" he screamed, clutching his face. "You broke my fucking nose, you cunt!"

One of the other roadies walked into the courtyard at that moment, pulled Preston away from me and walked him out back through the arches again and onto the street.

"You're bleeding." Alex whimpered beside me. "God, Johnny. I'm so sorry." He was starting to cry, and if I didn't stop it, he would break my heart into a million pieces for the pain that prick Preston had caused him. I pulled him in against me.

"Shhh. I'm a big lad, I'll survive." I laughed and kissed the top of his head.

"At least let me sort that cut for you," he said softly against my chest as he looked up at my face.

I felt a tingle in every damn inch of me when I looked

down and saw his face looking up at me. He was hurt, and I wanted to protect him. He was angry, and I wanted to soothe him. He was beautiful, and I wanted to kiss him. He stared at me, and I wanted to keep my arms around him, pull him to my lips, and anything else I felt like doing after that would just have to be done too.

And just like that, he blinked, pulled himself out of my arms, and the spell was broken. "Let me take care of that cut," he insisted, putting his hand in mine and pulling me to the rear entrance of the hotel.

―――――

RATHER THAN MAKING OUR WAY THROUGH THE HOTEL, Alex stopped a member of the reception team and got permission to use their back office. They delivered a first aid kit and ice to him. He set me on the chair in front of him and worked to sort the cut on my face.

He stood in the space between my legs and held my face between his hands. "It's started to swell."

His hands were soft on my skin, and I held my breath as he touched me. He removed his hands and moved to the first aid kit, straddling my left leg, pressing himself against me to reach the kit on the table behind me. Now *that* I felt everywhere, including in my cock, which was getting hard behind my jeans.

He ripped open the packet and touched the antiseptic wipe across my cheek. I hissed at the sting from the wipe, and he blew across the cut to help ease the irritation. That was about the only thing it eased. My cock was throbbing, and I had to sit on my hands to keep myself from reaching out and touching him. He leaned behind me again, and I almost groaned at the contact of him against me. This was fucking torture.

"This might sting again," he warned, and started to paint the liquid plaster over my cut.

"Jesus!" I grumbled when the cut burned under the fluid on my face. Again, Alex's breath graced my cheek as he once again blew over my face to take the sting off and to set the gel he'd painted on. I caught his gaze as he held my face still and worked his magic. The whole thing became hugely erotic. His breath on my face, his hands on me, his legs straddling my leg. I wanted to pull him down to sit on my lap. I wanted to pull his face to mine. I wanted to crush my lips to his. And in the split-second that it took me to consider it all, Alex did it for me.

His soft lips pressed hard against mine, and his tongue slid over my lips, seeking entry to my mouth. His crotch connected with my thigh, and I didn't need any more invitation to pull him hard against me and return his kiss full force.

His thigh pressed against my cock, and I moaned against his mouth. I ran my hands down over his back and grabbed handfuls of his gorgeous round arse. His hands moved from my face to my shoulders, his fingers digging into me as raw lust took over. I slid my hand from his arse to the leg he had between mine and encouraged him to move it and have him completely in my lap; I needed him to truly feel the effect he was having on me. He let me, and I pulled him hard against me when he was perched properly astride me.

I kept one hand on his arse and moved one up his back, under his t-shirt, caressing his back, side, and moving to the front, allowing me to press his pec against my hand. I could feel the hardness of his nipple against my palm, and I pried my mouth from his, letting my kisses rain down across his jaw and onto his neck. The soft, seductive sigh that bubbled out of him when my lips met the soft skin at the crease of his neck had me wanting to mark him. He was mine, and I wanted everyone to know it. I nibbled gently on his shoulder, and he moaned and squirmed in my lap. It was the only encouragement I needed to nip him harder. I was going to leave my mark on his skin and stake my claim.

Alex's fingers wrapped around my ponytail, tangling himself in my hair. He cupped the back of my head, holding me against his shoulder, encouraging me, his other hand still holding himself steady with my frame.

"Ohh, fuck, yes!" He sighed against my ear, grinding himself against my cock. I bit down harder on his shoulder, and he sank his short nails into my biceps. He was perfection. I had never needed anyone the way I needed this man.

From outside the door, I could hear Travis's voice. "They're just in the room down here?" he called.

"Shit!" Alex gasped, jumping from my lap and grabbing the first aid box from behind me just as the door swung open and Travis bounced in.

"Jesus, man. Look at your face. Are you okay?" he asked, glancing from me to Alex and back to me again. I glanced at him too; he looked like a kid who had just had his hand caught in the cookie jar. He blushed and moved towards the door.

"I'll just take their first aid kit back to the front desk," he announced as he moved past Travis. He put his arm up to stop him.

"Are you all right, Alex?" he asked.

He looked up at him and nodded. "I'll be fine. I'm just pissed off with Preston."

Travis's eyes scanned over him as if checking for injuries. His t-shirt was still hanging low on his shoulder. My mark was visible, and I knew he hadn't missed it.

"I think Dexter is looking for you. He's being all concerned big brother too." He smiled at him, and Alex disappeared out the door and it closed behind him.

Travis stared. "Well?"

"Well, what?"

"He has a fucking hickie. You're wearing skinny jeans, so I can see the massive stiffy you're sporting. Don't give me the 'what' bullshit!" He frowned. "You fucking promised, Johnathan! What the hell happened to you keeping your hands to yourself and your cock in your pants?"

I groaned. I was busted. I had kissed him, and I just couldn't control myself with Alex. "I'm sorry, mate. We had a pact, and I'm a dickhead because I didn't push him away when he kissed me."

"He kissed you?" His eyes widened. "Yeah, like you had nothing to do with it!"

I felt like a prize prick. I'd betrayed the promise I'd made to keep things strictly business between us all. Travis's hand slapped on my shoulder. "John, no offence, mate, but you're a walking cum machine, and I knew you would eventually cross that line."

I shook my head. "It wasn't me. He's the one who kissed me, twice!" I instantly regretted my comment, knowing I had given myself away. Travis's expression darkened.

"Twice? When the fuck was that?"

"Remember when the douchebag was in his house and smacked his brother?"

"Edinburgh? That was three fucking weeks ago, man!"

I shrugged. "It happened. I felt like a wanker about that, but I don't regret kissing him."

"You're a fucking idiot."

"That's what I thought you'd say. What's the point in

mentioning it, knowing you're going to chew my balls over it? It wasn't a mistake. I wanted to kiss him. Hell, I'd love to do a lot fucking more. But I can't, so I'm not going to, and there wasn't much point in discussing it with anyone, for his sake more than anything."

Travis understood. I could see that he did. Had I said anything, there would have been an awkwardness around Alex that he just didn't need when things were starting to really settle with him and Spitfire Junction. Travis shrugged. He couldn't fault my logic.

Travis squeezed my shoulder. "Promise me it won't happen again, and I'll say nothing if you don't. But I swear to fuck, if you don't keep your cock under lock and key, I'm going to fucking chop it off for you," he warned, and I nodded my agreement. We wouldn't speak of it, and we wouldn't let it affect our relationship with Alex.

# CHAPTER 14

## ALEX

Jesus fucking Christ. I had done it again. I kissed my bandmate. I was repeating the same mistake again. I had managed to avoid Dexter and head straight to my room. I didn't feel like trying to explain what happened. I knew the guilt was written all over my face.

I stood in the bathroom and looked at my flushed face staring back at me. "What the ever-loving fuck are you doing?" I asked my reflection. I felt like a slut. I felt like a brazen whore, and I wasn't sure I liked it.

I liked Johnny. I had felt something towards him, I had kissed him, and I had wanted to do much more. Now, here we were less than three weeks later, and the same thing had happened with him again. I wanted him. I wanted his lips on mine. I felt his cock through his jeans long before he had me sitting on his lap. He wanted to protect me, just like he had in Edinburgh, and it made me feel treasured, wanted, and like a precious jewel that he coveted.

I stripped off my clothes, turned on the shower, and stepped into the hot water. I thought it would heal me a little. I thought it would soothe me and make me feel better. Instead, it just increased the prickling through my skin. Every inch of me was on fire with need. Regardless of what I thought about myself for it, twice now, that incredible man had started something he hadn't finished. I was beyond horny and needed a release that felt like it would never come. I let my hands roam over my body. I caressed and kneaded my flesh before letting my fingers slip around my cock and attempted to give myself at least some relief.

———

When we all piled onto the tour bus to head for Rock City in Nottingham, I made sure to stay near the back, away from everyone else. I needed to hide; I had no idea how to handle the situation.

Johnny glanced in my direction when he got on, and I pretended to be looking out the window. I didn't know what to say to him. I didn't know what I wanted anymore.

Dexter bounced onto the bus in his usual bright and breezy mood. I looked up at him and he glanced at me, then at Johnny, and smirked. *Oh, fuck. He knows.* I could feel the heat creeping over my skin, feeling flushed. He looked at me with a knowing smile and headed directly for me. I guessed the next hour on the bus was going to be fun.

I tried not to make eye contact with Dexter when he sat down in front of me. I felt his eyes on me. He wasn't going to make any of this easy on me, and the longer I left it, the worse it got.

I managed ten minutes of trying to ignore him before my face felt too much like it was on fire, and I gave in and looked at him.

"You all right, Alex?" He grinned.

"I'm... yeah, I'm-I'm good."

"Johnny's face looks good today. Anything that makes Johnny Scott look more like a human being is to be applauded. Whatever you did seems to have helped." He smiled again.

"Cheeky fucker. I'm always gorgeous!" Johnny pouted from his side of the bus. Dex just smirked and glanced between us both. He said nothing more about it for the rest of the trip.

———

REHEARSALS HAD GONE WELL AGAIN, AND WE HAD ALL arrived back at the hotel for a bit of R&R before heading back to the venue for the gig. I was just walking down the hallway to my room when a hand grabbed my arm and pulled me into the housekeeping closet.

"Shhhh." The person, I quickly realised, was Johnny, whispering against my ear.

"Johnny?"

"Sorry, Alex. I didn't mean to scare you. I just wanted to apologise for my behaviour yesterday."

I blinked, taking in what he was saying. Was he apologising for kissing me? Or for sticking up for me? "I'm not sure what you think you need to apologise for," I replied, needing him to clarify.

"Going all caveman and punching people around you." He scrunched his nose up in a grimace.

"Oh, that. For a second there I thought you meant kissing me." I laughed without thinking about the words falling out of my mouth.

Johnny's hand held mine with a squeeze. "I don't regret that. I overstepped a line I really shouldn't have, but I don't regret it." My eyes focussed on his lips as he said the words. I felt a flush of heat over my skin as I thought about what it felt like to have them on mine.

"Stop looking at me like that, Alex, or we'll end up in trouble again."

A thrill went through me, and I couldn't help but keep my eyes locked on his lips; his full, beautiful, kissable lips.

"Fuck," he exclaimed, and his mouth captured mine, his hand at my jaw, pressing me back against the wall of the closet, his other hand grabbing me by the hip and pulling my body hard against his.

Electricity sparked through every nerve in my body at his possession of my mouth. I hungrily returned his kiss, needing more, wanting more, willing him to take it further than I dared.

I felt him, long and hard, pressed against my stomach, and the only thought that existed in my head in that moment was just how much I wanted to have him inside me. I flexed my hips against him, rubbing against his cock, making sure he had no doubts about what I wanted, or how hard he was making me in return.

In that split second, my mind let go of the reservations I should have had about being with Johnny again. I moaned against his mouth, even more turned on, thinking of how it would feel to have Johnny naked against me.

I panicked. I pushed Johnny back from me. "Stop," I begged breathlessly.

"Shit, Alex. I'm sorry..."

"Don't you dare say sorry!" I replied quickly. "I just need you to stop because, if you don't, I'm going to end up fucking you in a cupboard, and that's not really the kinda guy I want to be."

Johnny nodded, a slight smirk forming on his face. "You want to fuck me?" he asked boldly.

My cock twitched. "Yes." I blushed.

"I can take that for now." He smiled at me.

"I'm going to leave now, though."

He nodded. I moved past him, not taking my eyes off his, and headed out through the door of the closet.

Fuck. I wanted him.

# CHAPTER 15

## JOHNNY

Dammit, what the hell was wrong with me? I was getting on like a horny teenager, and worse still, I just couldn't seem to help myself around Alex. I had tried my best to keep my composure around him all day. I had stayed away from him. I had tried to make a little eye contact at least, just to make sure he was okay with me and it didn't seem like I was ignoring him. But he never looked at me once.

When Dexter got on the bus and started to talk to him, I couldn't help but think about Dex making him laugh, teasing and being friendly with him, and it just got me even more worked up. I was jealous, and it made me horny.

By the time we got back to the hotel, I couldn't take it anymore, and I had to get him alone and talk to him. I needed to know that we were still okay. I craved him, and the thought of having ruined any friendship with him or making him uncomfortable was more than I could take.

I didn't understand what it was about Alex that I was drawn to. I didn't know what it was about him that made me need to have him in my life. I had never felt like this about anyone before.

When he looked at my lips in that cupboard, I just had to have his mouth. I needed to taste his lips. I couldn't stop myself.

As much as I knew I needed to stop when he told me to, I hadn't wanted to. I needed to press against him. I needed to find my hands full of his arse. I needed to get him naked and find myself buried inside him.

I waited in that cupboard for a few minutes after he left, mostly because my hard cock trapped in my jeans made it particularly difficult to walk in a straight line. When I finally made it out of there, Dex was leaning on the wall right outside.

"Should I ask?"

"Uhhhh..." I hesitated, feeling like a kid caught doing what they had been told not to.

"Let's get a drink, and you can tell me what the fuck is going on with this band."

I knew he wasn't asking; he was telling me. I tried to figure out what I was going to say on our way to the bar. *Do I lie, or do I come clean? Fuck.*

# CHAPTER 16

## DEXTER

It wasn't like I didn't know exactly what was happening with the band. I had seen it all. I could read the body language of the three people I spent most of my time with very well. I could feel the sexual tension in the air between the two of them, and I knew something had to be going on.

Part of me just liked fucking with Johnny a little, but part of me really did want to know just how far this had all gone, and what risks it posed for the band and its future.

Johnny looked uncharacteristically like a man being led to the electric chair. I walked along beside him to the bar in silence. I knew my friend. If I was quiet and let his own mind do all the work for me, he would tell me everything.

We sat at the bar and I ordered us a Jack Daniels and Coke each, and again, I just waited.

"So..." Johnny started. I glanced at my friend and raised an eyebrow, waiting for his next comment. "It's not Alex's fault."

"What isn't?" I asked.

"It was me."

"You?" I said, keeping my tone even.

"I've kissed him, and... I mean, well, he's kissed me..." Johnny's face flushed.

*Damn, bruv. You really like him.*

"Is this going to be some sort of fucking game to you? You know you can't have him, so that just makes it all the more important to get the guy, and to hell with the band?"

Johnny knocked back his drink in one. "That's not what this is. I mean, I don't... well, I do, I want him, but not over the future of the band."

"And if he picks the band?" I asked.

Johnny grimaced and beckoned to the barman for a refill on his drink.

"You like him that much, huh?"

He nodded.

"From what I've seen, he likes you too."

He nodded again.

"You know I'm going to have to talk to Alex, and if we can't find a solution to this, I'm going to have to talk to Del. I don't want to be looking for another drummer again. Johnny, I can kinda understand. You're a walking testicle. But isn't it about time you grew the fuck up and stopped thinking with your cock?"

He knocked back his fresh drink and stood from his bar stool. "I know. I'm sorry," he said, then walked towards the lift and his room.

I lifted my phone and called Travis. "Mate, I'm in the bar. Where the fuck are you?" I asked. Typical Travis. He apologised and said that he'd be down in a few minutes. I hung up and waited for round two.

———

"WHAT THE FUCK IS JOHNNY PLAYING AT WITH ALEX?" I asked him when he sat down on the stool beside me and ordered a scotch.

"Johnny's after Alex?"

*Denial, huh? That's the gameplay we're going for?*

"You know only too well that Johnny has been attempting to get into his boxers," I stated.

Travis played with his glass, carefully considering his reply. "You had Johnny down here first, didn't you?"

I smirked. No flies on Travis.

"So, he probably told you everything, so you have me down here for what reason exactly?"

"Honestly, mate? I want to know what you think of all this. I mean, is Alex really worth ruining the band over?"

Travis didn't hesitate. "Johnny definitely thinks so, and that's not like him at all." He knocked back his scotch.

He was right. Doing anything other than just fucking a fella was so far out of character for our friend. We loved him, but the man was a whore until he met Alex. If I didn't know any better, I would have said that our friend was starting to fall in love with our new drummer.

# CHAPTER 17
## ALEX

I felt nervous the second I got to Johnny's hotel room door. I paused, and I was about to rethink knocking when the door opened and Johnny stood staring at me.

"Hi."

"Uh, hi," I mumbled.

"Come on in." He stepped aside to welcome me in, and timidly, I entered. I didn't know why I was so worried about being around him. Maybe it was because every time I caught him looking at me, it was starting to feel like I was his prey. The only thing was, I wanted to be his prey. I wanted to be devoured in the way his eyes hinted at.

"Can I get you anything?" He pointed to the minibar.

"No, thanks," I said, digging my hands into my jeans pockets to stop me from fiddling with the hem of my t-shirt and looking like a nervous idiot.

I watched as he pulled a chair out and placed it in front of me before sitting on the edge of the bed, facing me.

"Do we need to talk?" he asked, and I cleared my throat nervously.

"Yeah, I think we do," I said glumly, perching myself on the edge of the seat he had set out for me.

Johnny waited for me to start into whatever it was I was meant to be saying to him. I felt like a goldfish, my mouth opening and closing with the words not quite forming and allowing me to say anything. Johnny ran his fingers through his hair and hissed. "Spit it out then."

"Sorry." I grimaced. I knew I had to tell him we needed to cool it; I knew I needed to tell him we should stop whatever was developing between us because it was going to end so badly for me and the band if we didn't. But when I looked at his face, and the hint of pain on it, like he knew what was coming, I couldn't get the words out. Johnny glanced over at me with sadness in his eyes, and it cut me, leaving me feeling the sting in my heart. *Fuck.*

I tried to zone out and concentrate on the task at hand, but I knew that, no matter what I needed to say, I wouldn't be able to get those words out. Sure, it was the 'right' thing to do, but it wasn't what I wanted. It wasn't what he wanted either, from the look on his face, and I decided to tell him just that.

I stood in front of him and took a deep breath. "I came here to talk about what's been happening between us. I came here to say the things I think need to be said."

He looked up at me. "And what is it you think you need to say, Alex?"

I couldn't get another word out. I was drawn to him. Before I could think about it, I lowered my head, and my lips met his. A rush of pure lust washed over me, and I needed to kiss him hard. He needed to understand just how much I wanted him. His tongue danced with mine and his hands slid down by back, holding me, moving me back a touch before he stood and pulled me back hard against him.

Just like always with Johnny, my body cried out for more. I wanted more, and I was powerless to fight it. My body moulded against his. He grabbed my ass tight and I could feel the effect I was having on him pressed low against my stomach.

I tangled my hands in his hair, holding him against my mouth, not wanting the moment to stop. Breathlessly, Johnny pried his lips from mine.

"Damn, Alex," he breathed, his body pulling back from mine. Guilt and embarrassment flooded my senses.

"Shit, Johnny. I'm sorry..." I started, raising my hands to my face.

"For what? Coming here to dump me? Coming here to tell me that for the good of the band we need to part ways? And then kissing me instead?"

My mouth opened to answer, but the words wouldn't form. I wanted to tell him what I was thinking. I wanted to be honest.

Johnny stepped close, and my feet still wouldn't move.

"Say it then, Alex."

I shook my head. I couldn't. It wasn't what I wanted.

Johnny stepped closer still.

"I... can't. I know I should. I know it's messing up the band, and if you want to tell Dexter to replace me, I totally get it," I babbled, my head falling forward, my eyes finding the floor in shame.

Johnny's finger covered my lips to quiet me and swept under my chin to lift my head back up. "I don't think Travis and Dex would ever forgive me if I let you go. Besides, I happen to think you really are something special."

His mouth descended back onto mine, and he pulled me hard against him again. His tongue ran across my lips, demanding entry to my mouth. His hands felt warm spread out over my arse and kept me against his unmistakeably hard cock in his jeans.

My senses were on overload. Johnny thought I was something special. With everything that was happening with me and Preston, with the complete mess that this would make with the band, Johnny wanted me, knowing all that. And, Lord help me, I wanted him too.

Hungrily, I returned his kiss. I needed more. There was something liberating in the fact that Johnny knew everything and was so accepting. My hands found their way back to tangle in his hair, and my tongue danced with his, my hips moving against him.

Johnny's mouth broke free of mine. "Fuck, Alex. You're driving me crazy. But before we take this any further, I have to know. Are you sure this is what you want?" He studied my face, and I didn't want to deny it anymore.

I looked directly at him so he wouldn't doubt the sincerity of my words. "I want you."

A sexy little smirk snaked across his lips. "Absolutely sure?"

"Yes."

His grin said everything. Like all his Christmases and birthdays had come at once.

I blushed. I was overwhelmed that someone would be so interested in me. It also made my heart and stomach flutter.

"I don't want to be the reason your band breaks up, though," I told him, trying to stay rational.

"*Our* band will be just fine. You with us will be just fine," Johnny insisted. He took me by the hand and placed a kiss on my forehead. "As much as I want to take this further right now, I want you so much my cock aches, but I want to talk to Dexter and Travis first, and I want you to think about it all properly. Date me properly. I want you.

*Properly*." Johnny moved his lips back against mine for a soft and seductive kiss. I felt cherished as well as desirable. "Now, get the hell out of here before I can't resist the urge to taste every inch of you."

With my dick hard and throbbing in my jeans, my lips tingling, and my feet floating six inches off the floor, I left Johnny's room and headed to my own.

# CHAPTER 18

JOHNNY

I HAD JUST GIVEN MYSELF THE BIGGEST CASE OF BLUE BALLS I'd had since I was a teenager with a monstrous crush on my older sister's boyfriend.

I shook my head to try and clear the lust-fuelled fog that had taken over. I needed to talk to my bandmates and sort out the fact that I needed to date Alex.

I flopped down on the bed and roughly palmed my cock through the jeans holding it prisoner. Get a grip, Scott!

I groaned and rolled over to grab my phone from the bedside table.

*Need to talk to you mate. Bar in 10.*

I added Travis and Dexter to the recipients' list and hit send.

———

I WAS A FEW MINUTES LATE TO THE BAR; EVEN A COLD shower didn't really help to calm me down. Dexter and Travis were sitting at a table, away from everyone else. I guess they had a fair idea about why I wanted to see them, even if I didn't tell them why.

"Hey, Johnny," Dexter greeted, and Travis nodded in my direction as I approached.

"Alright, lads?" I said, pausing at the table. "Pints all right with everyone?" I asked, and with the approval of my friends, I headed to the bar.

"So, what's this all about?" Travis asked when I handed out the pints and set my ass down on the last seat at the table.

"It's about Alex," I started.

Dexter looked at me critically. "Are we going to like this?"

I shrugged. "Let's talk about it and find out, shall we?"

Travis studied me intently with a suspicious look.

"Okay, so, he came to my room, and he was going to tell me he was concerned about the band and that he wanted to cool it between him and me, because things have been a little horny of late, and... well, he couldn't, and I couldn't let him."

Travis's mouth fell open and Dexter just grinned.

"I fucking knew it!" Dex laughed. "I knew you liked him, and I knew you wouldn't be able to resist!"

Travis was more serious. "Do you like him? Is that what it is?"

"Relax, bruv," Dexter said, slapping his hand down on Travis's shoulder. "For the first time in his life, Johnathan Scott has found himself an ass that meant more to him that just a hole to fill."

Travis rolled his eyes and looked at me to confirm what Dexter had said.

"As much as it pains me to say these words, Dex is right," I reassured Travis. "I really do like him."

Travis took a swig of his pint, shocked.

Dexter smirked. "I'm proud of you, John. You actually have it in you to be a grown-up and have real feelings for someone."

I winced. I knew what he was saying was right. For the first time in my life, I cared about someone that wasn't me or my bandmates. I cared about a man in a way I had never had before.

I had to admit, this was going to be interesting.

# CHAPTER 19

## ALEX

I LAY IN THE BATH AND LET THE WARM WATER SOOTHE ME. I tried not to think about what Johnny had said. I didn't know if it was such a smart idea to be with him. I wanted to, but, God, was that something I could realistically do? There were so many what-ifs that were driving me crazy.

- What if it drove a wedge between the guys?
- What if it finished the band? Jesus, I would end up a pariah!
- What if it worked? Was this a 'for forever' relationship?
- What will the press say?
- Hell, what will Del say?

I closed my eyes with a sigh and tried to fight the spin cycle of possible scenarios going around in my head. It was all just too much. I sank lower into the water.

———

Dried and dressed, I decided food might be a good idea. A guy can't make sensible decisions on an empty stomach, right? I headed down into the lobby and out onto Broad Street. It was the reason we stayed in that hotel; there was so much choice right on the doorstep. Feeling lazy, I headed straight for Coast to Coast just across the street.

As soon as I walked in and glanced around the inner lower section of the restaurant, I regretted my choice. Sitting around a table were Johnny, Dexter, and Travis. In the split-second it took me to decide to turn around and leave, Johnny saw me.

I stood, frozen, as he got up from the table and strode towards me with purpose. "Alex," he greeted, pulling me hard against him in a hug.

"Hey, Johnny," I managed to squeak out.

"How did you know we were here?" he asked, loosening his grip.

"I didn't. I just went for the closest place."

Johnny grinned. "Then it's fate." He took my hand and pulled me towards my bandmates' table.

"Look who's joining us!" Johnny announced. He pulled out a chair in the corner beside him for me to sit on.

"Alex." Dexter grinned, and Travis smiled brightly in my direction. I felt my worries melt away in an instant. The looks on the faces of Johnny, Travis, and Dexter made me feel relaxed, safe, and cherished. Not only was the band where I belonged, but the three of them had started to feel like friends and family.

"Have you ordered?" I asked, trying to take my mind off the idea I kept feeling drawn to, that the little voice liked to point out to me, that I was making a mess for them all and was going to ruin everything.

*Fuck it. Just enjoy it all!*

Travis handed his menu to me. "Not yet. Have a look on there and decide what you want."

It was funny how loaded that statement felt. I toyed with the idea of telling them what I wanted wasn't actually on the menu. What I *really* wanted was Johnny. But my nerves got the better of me, and I buried my face in the menu.

The food came, the alcohol flowed, and I relaxed into the company around me. The guys told tales of funny moments that had happened on previous tours. They talked about Andy and how they had all met each other. They filled me in on almost all their history together. The good times. And then it was my turn.

"How did someone as hot as you ever end up with a slime ball like Preston Phillips?" Johnny asked.

Travis glared at him, and Dexter scolded him.

"No, It's okay!" I smiled. I felt comfortable and relaxed enough to tell them everything. Just like they had with me. "I met him when I was seventeen. He was in a band that played in a club I sneaked into a lot with my fake ID. He was twenty-eight when I met him. A real rock star, and I had the biggest crush on him. I couldn't believe it when he pulled me out of the crowd that night."

"I didn't know that about Preston," Travis stated.

"Know what?" Dexter asked.

"That the creepy bastard has always been toying with people way too fucking young for him."

"Not to mention too fucking good for him," Johnny added, watching me intently.

"If only I'd known that at the time." I sighed. "Mind you, without all that crap, I wouldn't be sitting here with any of you. So, I guess that's something to be grateful for, even if he is a massive prick."

Dex grinned at me and lifted his drink in a toast. "Amen to that!"

"To weird shit and awesome outcomes," Johnny added.

"To Alex," Travis chimed in.

Warmth radiated through my body. I was wanted. I was cherished. I belonged. "To Spitfire Junction," I added, glancing at each one of them in turn.

"To Spitfire Junction!" They all joined in, clinking their glasses with mine, all eyes on me as we took a drink.

# CHAPTER 20

## JOHNNY

I watched Alex relax with us and listened to him as he discussed everything that happened with him and the prick Preston. I took in the contented expression on his face and the genuine warmth he had towards me, Travis, and Dexter. There was no doubt in my mind that he was the right person, both the perfect fit for the band and the perfect fit for me. He might have been worrying about it and what it might or might not do with the band, but without a doubt, Alex Hart belonged with us. He belonged with me, and I wanted to make sure he knew just how much he was welcome and wanted as a bandmate by Dexter and Travis, and that and more by me.

Every time I looked at Alex, I felt it in more than just my cock. I needed to know that he was okay with being with me. Hell, I needed to convince him if he wasn't. I'd never needed a man in my entire life. I wasn't a complete wanker about it, I just never wanted to settle down, or to be with a man more than a handful of times. I'd never been in love and I'd never made a man any promises for anything beyond a good fucking. His pleasure was my only focus. But I already knew things could never be like that with Alex. He was worth so much more, and more was what I wanted to give him.

Dexter looked in my direction and gave me the faintest of nods. He knew what I was thinking. I could see the warmth in his own expression when he looked at our drummer, and I knew he understood. The nod, though, that was the boss's permission to do exactly what I was thinking.

Travis glanced at me too. A small nod came from his direction, and I knew he was also giving his permission for what was to come. Both my bandmates understood that I wanted to be with our drummer, and instead of talking me out of it, they took one look at me and agreed. I had their blessing. I didn't know what to do with myself next.

This was new territory to me.

———

The night rolled on, with more drinks, more food, and more good company.

Alex yawned. Dexter smiled and suggested I walk him back to the hotel.

"As long as you're sure?" Alex said.

Dexter nodded. "I'm sure. Don't worry about it. Travis and I will pay the bill."

Alex smiled and nodded. "Thank you all for a lovely evening. It has been wonderful. I really appreciate this. It was just what I needed."

We said our goodbyes, rose from the table, and headed back out onto Broad Street. Alex casually put his hands in his pockets as we walked the short distance back to the hotel.

"I've really enjoyed tonight," he said warmly.

"Me too. It's been nice to hear about your background. I'm sorry you had to deal with all of Preston's crap though."

His body stiffened a little at the mention of his ex's name. "Don't worry about it, Johnny. Like I said this evening, I wouldn't change it because it brought me here."

I smiled down at him and put my arm around him, pulling him in tight against me. He felt so good moulded against me, like he was made to fit perfectly with me. When he looked up at me, the expression on his face suggested he felt just the same.

Neither of us could find any words to express the moment that was happening between us, and instead, we walked through the lobby and into the lift in silence. In the small confines of the elevator car, the air began to feel charged, and I felt the same pull to him I had felt since the moment I met him.

I placed my hand at the small of his back and guided him along the corridor to his hotel room door. Suddenly, I felt out of my depth. Normally, I was cocky, and I could do this, but Alex was different. Normally, I would have been able to get in his boxers in a heartbeat, but this wasn't just about getting in his bed. This was about me expressing my feelings for someone, and I'd never done that before.

We paused outside his door, and he turned to face me, looking up at me expectantly. Every single signal he sent me told me just how much he wanted me. Just how much he needed this to happen, and just how much he was mine for the taking. And I acted like a complete pussy. My lips met his softly and briefly. I told him goodnight, and I turned and walked away, leaving us both unsatisfied.

I didn't dare turn around. I didn't think I could bear the look on his face. Instead, I hid out in my room and made sure nobody knew about my failure.

# CHAPTER 21

## ALEX

And just like that, he left. I was so dumbstruck I stood there for a moment, watching him as he disappeared back down the corridor, wondering what the hell just happened. Didn't he want me? Didn't I make it clear enough that I wanted him? Whatever it was, something had gone wrong, and this wasn't the ending to the evening I had expected.

I opened the door to my room, walked inside, and threw myself down onto the bed. My mind ran over the circumstances of the evening. Had I missed something? Had I done something wrong? Or was it just plain and simple; Johnny didn't want me? Had Preston been right about me. Was I just not enough?

Rather than dwelling on it too much, I decided to take a shower and wash my blues away. The only problem was, while standing under the warm water, my troubles weren't washed away, they were merely amplified. All I could think about was Johnny's hands on my skin, Johnny's lips on mine, and that did nothing to make me feel any less of a failure. For a split second, my mind went to the place I didn't want it to, and I thought about the comments Preston had made about me and my body. The comments that had made me feel like nothing. The comments that told me that nobody would ever want me. Feeling forlorn, I left the shower, put on my favourite comfy pyjama bottoms, and climbed into bed.

Sleep was not my friend. I just couldn't settle myself to get there. By the time three a.m. came around, I couldn't take it anymore, and I had to get up. It wasn't long before I found myself heading down the corridor to Johnny's room.

*What the hell are you doing?* The only thing I could think of was getting him to realise I had wanted him. I paced up and down outside his hotel room door. I tried to talk myself out of it. I tried to tell myself I could talk to him about it tomorrow, but something just wouldn't let me leave it alone.

I knocked on his door and waited. I heard him mumbling inside, and the door opened to reveal him rubbing his bleary eyes in just a pair of boxers. "What?" he asked sleepily.

"Shit, sorry. Did I wake you?" I asked, feeling stupid, knowing the answer already.

"Alex?" he asked softly when he realised it was me banging on the door at such a ridiculous time of night. "Are you okay?"

"Can I come in?" I enquired, my voice subdued.

Johnny moved out of the way of the doorway to allow me to enter. I jumped a little when the door closed behind me, my nerves kicking in to overdrive. "I have something I need to say," I told him. He slumped back on the bed, regarding me with curiosity. "I couldn't sleep. I needed to... I mean... I..." I stuttered and started to pace again.

Johnny watched me struggling to express myself, and

when I paced past him for the fourth time, he grabbed my arms and stopped me in my tracks.

"Whatever it is, you can tell me," he said reassuringly. I bit my lip and nodded.

*You're a big boy, Alex. You can do this.*

"I need you to tell me to be sensible because I know I'm not. It's just that, I have these feelings..." I began. Johnny's eyes widened, and I worried this was going to ruin everything, but I just couldn't make my mouth stop. "I like you. And you and I kissed, and I wanted more, and I thought you did too, until tonight when you just left, and I needed to come here and say it. I needed to tell you I *like* you, and I want more. But I know it's crazy and I know you need to tell me now that I'm being silly. You need to tell me to stop." My brain ran away with me, and the words just kept pouring from me. I was having the worst case of verbal diarrhoea possible.

I looked at Johnny, willing him to say something. Willing him to tell me I was crazy. Instead, he stood, towering above me, looking down at me intently. I couldn't move, and I gasped when I realised what he was doing. His lips crushed against mine, and he held me hard against him. Lust overwhelmed me, and all I wanted was more.

# CHAPTER 22

## JOHNNY

I'D NEVER BEEN A MAN TO LOOK A GIFT HORSE IN THE mouth. Alex was in my room at three in the morning, and he was confessing to wanting me. To liking me; *really* liking me. He was being kept awake thinking about it. Hell, he actually thought I didn't want him; that I needed to fix. Not another second could pass with him thinking I didn't want him. I did the only thing I could think of to let him know what I was thinking.

I stood, invading his space. He didn't move; he was rooted to the spot. I pressed against him and crushed my lips to his before he had the chance to make me stop.

My tongue darted along the line of his lips, begging them to part, needing him to accept what I was giving him. I tried not to think too much about what I really wanted to give him, but standing in front of him in just my boxers, I think it was pretty obvious what I wanted to give him and the effect he was having on me.

Alex moaned against my mouth and his hands ran over my back. His hands felt so good against my skin, and my prick bobbed against his stomach. I couldn't think of anything or anyone I had ever wanted more. It was all about Alex.

*God, this isn't enough.* I needed him to know just how much he meant to me and I couldn't tell him yet. The words just didn't want to come, so I did the only thing I could do. I showed him.

My hands slid down his body to his ass, and I grabbed him, pulling him hard against me. He grabbed at my back and his tongue duelled with mine. I kissed him so hard that it made me dizzy. He was so tight against me it felt like we were about to become one, two halves of the same whole, and God help me, but my heart fluttered at the thought.

Breathlessly, our lips parted, our foreheads still touching. "That's not telling me I'm being silly," he murmured against my lips.

"Why the fuck would I tell you that?" I asked. I scooped him up in my arms, turned, and set him down gently on the bed. "I think this is the best idea you've had since I've met you." I stalked up his body, coming to rest naturally between his thighs and claiming his mouth again with mine.

Our kiss was hard, hot, and filled with all the tension that had been building between us for weeks. Alex hooked his leg over mine and his hips moved against mine. His body begged me for more. I knew he was seeking the relief I needed to bring him.

I allowed my mouth to roam from his. I traced the outline of his jaw in tiny kisses, nibbling when I got to the tender skin at the join between his shoulder and neck. His hands found their way to the skin on my back again, and the harder I sucked on his shoulder, the more his nails grazed at my flesh. A moan rumbled through his body, and one of his hands pulled on my hair.

"You okay?" I asked when he tugged on my locks for a second time.

He sighed and licked his lips as he looked up at me. "I'm getting there," he breathed in reply while he flexed his hips against me again, trying to tempt me into more.

"Ah! Ah! Ah!" I scolded with a smirk. "I'm taking my time with you, Alex. I won't be rushed."

He groaned and rolled his eyes at my comment.

I dipped my head to his chest and nuzzled against it through his t-shirt. My mouth covered his already pert nipple, and I sucked on it, nibbling it through its cotton covering. Alex's hands twisted into my hair again. I slid my hand under the material and ran my fingertips over his other nipple as I continued to tease him with my hot breath and teeth.

I felt like a teenage boy playing with the first human body he'd ever been allowed near. He flexed and shifted beneath me, and I could feel how hard he was for me. I wanted to touch him. I wanted to let him know what I was feeling by having my hands and mouth all over him, but I really did need to savour every last second of our first time together.

I moved my weight over him in such a way where I could get both hands on his chest without totally crushing him. I pulled on the bottom of his t-shirt and encouraged him to pull it over his head and off. His toned form with just a smattering of hair lay bare before me. God, I could have died right then and gone a very happy, yet unsatisfied man.

With him naked from the waist up in front of me, I just couldn't help myself. I needed to get my hands on him. I needed to touch and kiss every inch that lay exposed before me before I worked my way to other wonders I needed to feast on.

I teased and tempted him with my mouth and hands. I kissed and caressed his shoulders, his chest, and over his stomach. His breathing quickened, his hips flexed against me, and the look on his face told me he needed more relief than I was ready to give him.

I returned my mouth to his and drank him in hungrily, my hand still rubbing over his skin. I couldn't take it any longer, though. It just wasn't enough. I slid my hand down over his stomach to his waistband, wriggled my fingers beneath it, and caressed a trail down over his rock hard cock.

# CHAPTER 23
## ALEX

Fucking hell, this man was a tease, and he bloody well knew it. But it felt so damn good to finally be giving in to my feelings for him. Every inch of my skin was heated. His touch and his mouth were turning me on and making me crave more.

When his hand slipped beneath my pyjama bottoms, I gasped. My cock twitched in anticipation of what was to come, and I needed to have him inside me.

The man was pure sex, just as I fantasised he would be. He smelled incredible, and he knew exactly what to do to drive a man crazy. His skin felt so good under my fingers, and the way he turned me on with his hands and mouth was just breath-taking.

I moaned against his mouth when his finger finally slid between my buttocks. His mouth left mine. "Jesus. I need to be inside you, Alex," he commented, his mouth back on mine a second after, and his fingers sweeping over my arse-hole in teasing, soft strokes.

*Oh, fuck. This man is going to be the death of me.*

I let the intensity of the lust I was feeling wash over me.

He moved his hand to his mouth and licked a finger before returning it between my legs. He slid one of his long fingers deep into my ass with very little effort.

It was too much. My eyes rolled back in my head in pleasure, and my mouth opened in an excited sigh. "Oh, fuck, Johnny!" I breathed. He took that as his invitation to do just what I was hoping he would. His mouth latched onto my exposed nipple, and he curled his fingers deep inside me. I tangled my hand in his hair and held him against me as his fingers thrust in and out of me, and he kept pausing to tease my P-spot.

I felt it building within me. That fluttering low in my stomach, that tingling straight through my taint and into my balls. "Oh, God, Johnny. I'm going to come."

He pinched my nipple a little harder, and his fingers curled again against that soft spot deep in me. I closed my eyes and arched my back, the waves of my orgasm hitting me like a tsunami.

As my eyes came back into focus, I was delighted with the sight of Johnny licking his finger.

"Fuck, you taste so good." He grinned at me.

I just smiled at him. It had been a very long time, if ever, that I had had such a reaction with a man. But it wasn't enough; not yet. I stared at his lips as they glistened because of his finger, because of me. I wanted to taste myself on them. I wanted to feel them on me where his fingers had been.

Emboldened, I told him exactly what I thought he should be doing. "You should taste more of me. I need your mouth on me."

"You're exactly right," Johnny replied. He dipped his head to kiss me, letting me taste myself on his lips and tongue, and then he disappeared, blazing a trail of sweet kisses down my body. He pulled on my pyjama bottoms and encouraged me to shimmy out of them, leaving me exposed to him.

One touch of his hand against my inner knee was sufficient enough to encourage me to spread my legs for him, letting him feast on the full view of what lay between my thighs.

"Jesus, Alex. You are glorious," he told me, shifting his weight to settle between my legs. "I need to have my cock deep inside here, but not before I have you coming on my tongue."

The thought of that alone was enough to make me moan before Johnny even touched me. His tongue traced lightly along the length of my taint, teasing me and tempting me before he finally let his tongue sweep over my balls and my cock. Johnny lapped at me before his tongue finally settled on the head of my prink, his lips wrapped around it, and he sucked it gently into his mouth.

A long, slow moan sounded from my lips.

"Fuck, yes, Johnny."

The delicious pressure he was applying was bringing me closer and closer to the brink of orgasm again. He sucked my dick deep into his mouth until I felt it hit the back of his throat. He so expertly sucked and licked me until I knew that it wasn't going to be long before I came.

Johnny seemed to know just what was about to happen, and as I was about to climax, he slid two long digits back inside me. A tidal wave of feelings washed over me, and I came hard again.

Johnny's fingers paused in their actions, but his mouth didn't stop. The gentle sucking continued as he waited for the pulsing to subside around his fingers. He swallowed every drop that I had to give him, and with his fingers working their magic once again on my p-spot, it wasn't exactly the smallest load of cum. Once Johnny was sure my orgasm was finished, he lifted his mouth briefly. "Holy shit you're so fucking sexy, Al. You taste fucking amazing, and I can't take it anymore," Johnny told me as he lifted his head from between my legs. "I need to be inside you now."

He didn't wait for me to say anything, he just moved from the bed, slipped out of his boxers, and looked at me expectantly. For a moment, I was stunned. The sight of Johnny completely naked and incredibly erect was infinitely better than what I had ever pictured in my imag-ination.

"Better grab the lube from my bedside table," Johnny instructed.

I didn't hesitate to lean over, open the drawer beside the bed, and lift out the lube that was in there. I lay back, exposed, handed him the bottle, and watched him intently. Despite everything we had just done, I felt suddenly quite vulnerable.

Johnny seemed to pick up on it. "Hey, no need for that look. I can't wait to feast on everything I see." He cracked open the lube, rubbed it all over his cock, and crept over the bed and over me.

His mouth descended back over mine, and I drank him in. I tasted my spunk on his lips, and that only got me hotter. I wrapped my arms around his neck and held him against me. His tongue traced over my lips and dipped softly between them. I moaned against them. He was taking his time. He was making sure he savoured the moments between us, and he made sure I was taken care of and satisfied.

"God, you are beautiful," he murmured against my lips before moving back to my chest again. He sighed, taking a nipple in his mouth and sucking on it languidly. "You," *kiss,* "are," *kiss,* "amazing," *kiss,* "Alex." *Kiss.* He told me as he swept across my stomach, punctuating every word with a butterfly-like touch.

My heart flipped in my chest. I wanted him. I really wanted him, and I needed it to be more than just sex. He was filling up my chest with a flood of emotions.

"Johnny," I pleaded.

He looked up at me and smirked, stalking his way back up to my mouth, sliding himself in between my legs, his cock lined up perfectly with the entrance to my arse.

"What do you want?" he breathed against my lips.

"I want you," I told him.

"Where do you want me?"

I moaned in need. He knew only too well what I wanted and where I wanted it. "You need me to say it?" I asked.

"Say it." He shifted his hips so that the head of his rock-hard cock teased against my ready asshole, ready to sink into me.

It emboldened me. "I want you to take your deliciously hard cock and slide it as deep into me as you can get it."

Johnny moaned, crushed his lips to mine, and in one slow roll of his hips, sank his cock deep into my ass, sheathing himself completely in my warmth.

# CHAPTER 24

## JOHNNY

I couldn't help myself. I needed it more than I needed him to ask again. When he came in my mouth, my cock was so hard it was painful. I needed to sink deep inside him, and I couldn't take another minute. His delicious and oh-so-ready arsehole was all I could think of. This wasn't like it had ever been before for me. I was never consumed with the need for a fuck. I liked it, sure. Hell sometimes froze over and I would even enjoy the same arsehole more than once, but this was something completely different.

When he looked me right in the eyes and told me what he needed from me, I couldn't resist. He was mine, and he needed to know how much I would worship him for however long he would let me. He had to know I was his.

I moaned against his mouth when I finally slid my cock inside him, and his legs went straight around me to keep me where I was. I rolled my hips in slow circles. This wasn't fucking, this was making love. He was going to feel special. He was going to feel incredible. He was going to know just how much I cherished him and wanted him.

Alex moaned against my lips and I kissed down along his neck, over his collarbone, and back to his nipples. His back arched, and he gasped in pleasure when I locked my mouth around his nipple and flicked my tongue over that stiff little peak. I held myself off him with one elbow and allowed my hand to caress his side while I flexed my cock against that little soft bundle just inside his asshole again. His hips lifted against me, his breathing picked up, and the sounds that were erupting from him were just fucking incredible.

*Sweet fuck. I want to stay deep inside his glorious asshole forever.* I picked up the pace with my hips. I knew that because of all the stimulation he'd had already, he was unlikely to come again for me, but I couldn't hold back anymore. I started to thrust harder and faster into him. I shifted my weight to the other elbow and lapped at his other nipple. I moaned against him as I felt him clench around me.

I knew that prostate stimulation was capable of what could feel like multiple orgasms, but Jesus, I'd never seen it or felt it in person until then.

"Oh, fuck, yes, Alex. Come hard for me," I encouraged, catching him looking at me as I did. I locked his gaze with mine and made sure he knew not to look away. I wanted, hell, I needed that connection with him. I needed to see him coming again for me, and I needed him to see the effect he had on me, how he was making me come undone, and it was all for him.

The sound of our voices echoed around the room as I pounded into him, furious to find release, to make that connection with him. I could feel his orgasm building again, and this time, I wanted to come right along with him. I thrust into him faster and harder, chasing that peak, and just as I felt him clench around me again, my balls tightened and I exploded into him with a roar.

I dropped my head against his chest as I waited for my breathing to calm and my heart rate to go back to normal. For the first time in my life, I had made love to a man I had feelings for. He absently ran his fingers through my hair as he waited for his own body to calm down.

"You just came inside me," he said softly.

*Fuck!*

I lifted my head and looked at Alex. He wasn't pissed at me, but I was so damn angry at myself. "Shit," I snapped and went to move off him.

Alex held on to me to keep me where I was, still inside him. "Don't you dare move. It's okay. I wouldn't have it any other way," he told me, his hand stroking over my face.

"I'm so sorry. I just couldn't help myself."

He smiled genuinely at me. "It's not like you were the only one in the room, John. I took that risk right along with you." He wrapped his arms around me, pulling me tight against him.

We stayed wrapped up together until my arms couldn't take it anymore. We showered together, then curled up in bed beside each other and fell fast asleep.

# CHAPTER 25

## DEXTER

When I saw Alex and Johnny the next morning, I didn't need to ask what had happened between them; it was written all over both of them.

Alex looked contented and confident. Johnny looked a weird mix of smug and happy. This wasn't my friend's usual post-hook-up look; this really had been something else. Alex's smile was warm and genuine when he greeted me. "Morning, Dexter."

"Morning, you." I grinned. "You've clearly done something that agreed with you!" I teased, watching as a blush started on his neck and chest and quickly crept over all of his face. "Are you joining us for breakfast before we go?"

He shook his head. "Heading out for a run before we move on."

I watched as he walked away from us, heading for the lobby and the main entrance, and that last little look over his shoulder towards Johnny before he left. *Oh, yeah. Something definitely happened.*

"What's that about?" I enquired, looking at Johnny.

He shrugged. "Dunno, mate."

Johnny's poker face game was strong, but there was just one problem. I *knew* it was his poker face. He was hiding something, and I would bet my right bollock that Alex was hiding the same thing. *Interesting.*

"Uh-huh," I muttered, letting Johnny know full well that I didn't believe him. "Did something happen between you and Alex?"

Johnny looked up at me. "A gentleman never tells."

*Well, that's new.*

"You've never been a gentleman, John," I reminded him.

He shrugged and stayed silent. *Wow.* Something had happened. Something of importance to Johnny. Something he wanted to protect.

Travis interrupted my thoughts and joined us for breakfast.

"I'm going to assume from the look on both your faces that shit happened between Johnny and Alex?"

Johnny just looked at our friend. I rolled my eyes. "Our boy is keeping schtum, so I think it's safe to say 'yes'," I informed Travis.

Travis looked at Johnny, studying him closely before smirking a little and lifting the menu to decide what he was going to get for breakfast. It seemed Travis could see the glaringly obvious thing that was written all over Johnny's face; he was very much smitten with Alex, and something had very clearly happened between them.

---

"He really does like him then?" Travis laughed beside me as we started to load our gear into the bus and get ready to move on to the next town.

"Seems like it, Trav." I smiled.

"That's definitely not like him, is it?" Travis raised an eyebrow.

He was right. It wasn't anything like the Johnny that we had come to know, but it was bloody heart-warming to see. It also looked like Alex was very much into Johnny as well. I knew that, if I had pulled my friend aside, he would have done everything in his power to stop this all from happening, and no doubt beaten himself up endlessly when the inevitable had happened and he hadn't been able to pump the brakes on whatever was between him and Alex.

So instead of beating him up over it, I decided that the better idea was to leave it alone and let my friend go with these new feelings of his. I just hoped it would be okay in the end and wouldn't blow up in the band's face. Of any of us falling in love at any time ever, I didn't see it being Johnny.

# CHAPTER 26
## ALEX

I took my customary favourite spot at the back of
the bus. Johnny just smiled at me and looked away every
time I glanced in his direction. It was like being a teenager
and giggling every time your crush looked at you.

Travis made his way down to where I was sitting and
took the spot opposite me.

"You missed breakfast," he said.

I looked up from the book I was reading. "I did. I
wanted to get a run in before putting my arse back on this
bus for a few hours."

"So, you and Johnny, huh?"

I felt my cheeks flush with heat. The second I thought
about what happened with Johnny, I wanted to squirm in
my seat. A mixture of lust and self-consciousness flooded
my senses.

"You're blushing. It gives you away," Travis said softly. I
looked up at him and felt eyes on me, glancing over and
catching Johnny looking at me. I'm sure I blushed some
more. That man was definitely going to be the death
of me.

———

A couple of hours later, the bus pulled up outside the Hilton in Cardiff. The next night, we would play in The Globe. As I bent over to pull my bag out of the bus, Johnny stepped in behind me, right against my backside, his hands finding my hips. "You okay with that? Want me to carry it for you?" he asked.

I looked at him over my shoulder. "It's all good," I said, smirking at him and shaking my head.

Travis stepped into the space, took my bag from me, and headed to the front door of the hotel. "Put him down, Johnny." He laughed as he disappeared through the door.

Johnny's hands gripped at my hips before they dropped to his sides. "Spoilsport," he grumbled as he looked to where Travis had entered the hotel. I rolled my eyes and laughed, grabbed my other bag, and escaped to the hotel entrance.

———

Once rehearsals were over, I went back to my room. I was starting to feel a bit queasy, and a lot exhausted. I planned to just vegetate in my room, watch crap reality shows on TV, and eat junk via room service. I had just dressed in my boxers after a shower and was browsing the room service menu when there was a knock at my room door.

I sighed and plodded over to look through the spyhole. Johnny stood on the other side. I pulled the handle and swung the door wide. There he stood, Domino's pizza box in his hand, and a little brown paper bag hanging underneath.

"Hey."

"Hey, Alex. I thought you might be in need of comfort food?" he asked with a smile.

I smiled at him. "That would be awesome. Thank you," I said, moving back to let him come in. He strode in, set the pizza and bag on the bed, kicked off his shoes, and sprawled himself over the bed, looking amazing as usual, even in just jogging bottoms and a t-shirt.

"What flavour?" I asked as I closed the door and headed over to the bed to join him.

"New Yorker, with added red onions and peppers."

*My favourite.* He knew what I liked, and I was suitably impressed.

"There's Ben and Jerry's Caramel Chew Chew in the bag, and a few ice-cold Cokes too." He smiled and grabbed a slice, taking a huge bite.

"Someone's been paying attention." I smiled.

He shrugged. "You make it easy to pay attention."

My stomach fluttered, so did my heart, and I grabbed my own slice of pizza and settled myself on the bed beside Johnny.

"Are you going to watch this shit? Really?" he asked, lifting the remote control.

"Uh, yes. You should see some of the weird shit these two have to fix after terrible surgery."

"Isn't he married to some crazy woman in one of those housewife shows?"

"He is, and the other one was. Would you like to watch something else instead?" I smiled.

"Hey, it's your room, your TV," he said, holding up his hands in defeat. "But, hell yes. I don't watch this shit." He laughed.

I lifted the cushion from behind me and swatted him with it. "Shit, is it?" I asked. The look on his face was priceless when the pillow made contact with the back of his head.

"Oh, it's like that, is it?" He laughed, closing the lid of the pizza box and setting it on the floor beside him. In a split second, Johnny grabbed my hips, slid me closer to him, and started tickling my sides.

"Ahhh! NO!" I cried out, squirming under his touch, too ticklish for this to be a fair fight. I pushed at him, trying to get him off me, laughing as I did.

"Yeah. Not so clever now, is it?" He laughed at me. "Hitting a poor, defenceless man with a cushion!"

As I squirmed and tried to push his hands away, he grabbed my wrists with one of his hands and pinned them above my head. When he did, his stance was more over me than beside me. I looked up at him, and he looked down at me, and the reality of the situation dawned on us. Johnny was pressed against me. I was breathless, and my hands were pinned above my head. Before I could say anything or catch my breath, Johnny's mouth crushed against mine.

His tongue plundered my mouth, and I let it dance with my own. The hand he had been using to tickle me found its way around my waist, kneading into my flesh.

I moaned against Johnny's lips. He was hot and heavy, and my head was spinning. This wasn't what I had expected from him, but now I knew this was what he was like, I couldn't get enough.

I tugged my hands, needing him to let me go. I needed to get my hands on him. I needed to feel his skin under my fingertips. Johnny conceded and freed my wrists.

I grabbed fistfuls of the back of his t-shirt, pulling it, trying to pull him tighter against me. I kissed him back hard with everything I had.

His thumb and finger pulled on my nipple, twisting it a little before returning to grabbing my waist roughly. The man was demanding as hell, and I just wanted more and more. He moved his mouth from my mine over my jaw to my neck, where he started to nibble. Dear God, all I wanted was for him to properly nip at my neck and leave me marked. He was turning me into a feral little hellcat who just couldn't get enough.

I slid my hands under his t-shirt, my nails grazing his back.

"Fuck." He moaned into my neck, his hot breath turning me on even more. He lifted his head and looked at me. "Are you okay?"

I nodded.

"Are you hard for me?" he teased, knowing full well from the tenting that was going on in my boxers that I was indeed rock hard for him. I moaned and squirmed beneath him; he knew I was, but it made it all the more arousing because he wanted me to say it.

"Are you hard for me, Alex?"

I caught his gaze and held it before I replied. "Yes, I am."

"Oh, fuck, yes!" His tongue circled my hard nipple and his hand continued to knead my flesh.

I knotted my hand in his long plait and held his head against my chest.

"Oh, God. Johnny, I need you inside me."

I watched him smile around my nipple, and he sucked even harder. He shifted his weight to get between my thighs. It was like I had issued him a request and he instantly needed to comply.

"I think you have too much on," he said, raising an eyebrow suggestively.

"I could say the same thing about you."

"That's easily fixed." He hopped back off the bed. I watched in awe as he pulled his t-shirt slowly over his head, revealing his body little by little. His toned form was a work of art; he was making my cock painful the more of himself he revealed.

"Your turn," he said, dropping his t-shirt to the floor.

I lifted my hips and followed his example, slowly teasing my boxers down over my thighs and calves and casting them to the floor.

Johnny's green eyes shone darker and sparkled with lust. "Christ, you are delicious."

I bit my lip and smirked at him. "You're quite the feast yourself."

He grinned and pulled a body-building pose. "Why, thank you." He winked.

"Poser!" I laughed.

Instantly, Johnny's hand was around my ankle, and he yanked me down the bed as I yelped in surprise.

"Poser? How's this for posing?" he asked as he pulled me to sit up and yanked his boxers down to his ankles.

The air left my body in a rush as I came face to face with Johnny's huge cock for the first time. My mouth opened, and he pressed his thumb into my mouth, testing me out. I looked up at him, wrapped my lips firmly around the digit, and sucked, running my tongue over the pad.

"Jesus Christ!" He pulled his thumb from my mouth with a pop and slid his hand to the back of my head. His look told me everything he wanted. I opened my mouth wider, and while staring right at him, took the head of his cock into my mouth.

He had the biggest dick I had ever had the pleasure of getting my tongue against. My jaw was going to ache after this, but when I saw the look on Johnny's face, I knew it would be completely worth it. Lust and appreciation shone on his features, and when I pushed him farther back into my mouth, his eyes closed, and his head fell back.

"Fuck!"

I ran my tongue over the underside of his cock, rolled it over the head a few times, and then sank back down over him again, attempting to get him a little farther in again. I teased him in and out of my mouth, repeating the action and watching his reaction each time. Soon, he was tightening his grip on my hair and pushing my face down on his length a little more. He was making me gag on him, and it was turning me on like crazy. I wanted to please him. I wanted to give into his silent demands for more. I wanted him to fuck my mouth. I needed it.

My hands stroked over his thick, hairy thighs. I let one hand skim across the bottom of his balls.

"Oh, FUCK!"

His hand gripped my hair so tightly, and his stance widened just a little to let me stroke along between his legs. I cupped his balls and let my fingers trace over the skin between his arsehole and his scrotum. Every time I approached his ass, he moaned a little more. Daringly, I let my finger slide right back until it was over his arsehole and I rubbed hard against the ring of muscle. His hips bucked, his legs widened again, and he looked down at me with an intensity that practically set me on fire.

Feeling brave and emboldened, I pushed the tip of my finger in against the resistance of his arsehole. It allowed me to enter him, and he groaned loudly.

"Oh, Jesus, Alex! Yes! I'm going to come." He loosened his hold on my hair. "If you don't want it in your mouth..." His voice trailed off before he could finish that thought. I sucked him that little bit harder and faster and started to finger his ass as I did.

Johnny's cock twitched in warning of what was to come. His breathing was fast, and his delicious sounds echoed around the room.

"Oh, God!"

His voice was deep and blissful, and his cum started to spurt out into my mouth and down my throat. I felt triumphant. *I did that.* He was unloading into me, giving me everything he had, and I lapped up and swallowed every drop greedily, pulling my finger from him as I did.

Johnny's hand traced from the back of my head along my jaw and tilted my head up to look at him again, freeing his cock from my mouth as he did. He bent and kissed my mouth softly; a silent thank you. His tongue traced over my lips to the last of his cum that I hadn't been able to lick off yet.

"Mmmm..." he murmured as cleaned it off me. "Your turn."

# CHAPTER 27

## JOHNNY

My head was floating. Jesus. Alex had just given me the best experience of my life, and I wanted more than anything to taste him in return. I kissed him and enjoyed my own flavour on his tongue. But I knew he tasted so much sweeter.

I pulled him up onto his feet and kissed him. My hands ran down over his body, found his buttocks, and cupped them in my hands. He kissed me back softly, with an underlying hint of need and hunger.

I wrapped an arm around his back and scooped him up with another arm under his legs. "Thank you," I said, as I carried him back to the bed, kissed him on the nose, and laid him on his back.

I let my eyes roam over Alex hungrily. He really was a sight to behold. Perfect in all the right places. While he was a good bit shorter than me, he was still perfectly proportioned, with long legs to fit his stature. God, I wanted them wrapped around me as I pounded into his delicious little hole.

I kept my eyes on him as I moved back to the bottom

of the bed. I stood there for a moment, watching him, daring him with my eyes, challenging him to say what he wanted and needed. Instead, he let his hand caress slowly over his torso, right to his stiff prick, and gave it a stroke.

I smirked and stalked up the bed over him like he was prey. I lifted his leg from the bed and wrapped my mouth around his big toe, sucking it into my mouth, running my fingers up either side of his calf. I kissed every other toe on the same foot, and when I took his big toe into my mouth for a second time, he gasped, and the fact that his hips gyrated against his hand did not go unnoticed by me.

"Your feet are very sexy," I told him as I set down one foot and picked up the other. I lavished the same attention over it and watched as it evoked the same response from him. Instead of a gasp, he moaned this time. His thighs parted a little and his cock bobbed as it throbbed in need.

"Johnny," he pleaded.

"All in good time, Alex." I grinned and lowered myself between his legs and started to kiss my way up from his right ankle to his knee. Once I reached his knee, I moved back to his left ankle and started again.

Every single inch of his skin smelled and tasted divine, and my spent cock was already coming back to life. I felt so alive perched between his legs, paying him all the attention I had in my heart to give him, and that was exactly where Alex was for me. He was under my skin, driving me crazy, and making my heart swell. I wanted to ravish him every day, and if that was every day for the rest of my life, that would be the most amazing thing that could ever happen to me. More than the band. More than the fame. It was most definitely all Alex.

I slid a little farther up the bed, delighting in the fact that he willingly spread his legs wider to let me in against him. I kissed feather-light kisses along both of his thighs and gazed up at him. He was biting his lip and staring down at me, looking like a vision of wanton beauty. "Tell me what you want," I demanded.

"You."

"Where do you want me?"

He closed his eyes, as though he was summoning the courage to tell me.

"Inside me," he breathed out. "God, I need you inside me."

I didn't need any more invitation than that, and I sank my mouth down over his cock and swept my tongue along his length. The taste of his pre-cum flooded my senses, and I couldn't help but moan against his cock.

"Holy fuck, you taste amazing," I breathed, and swept my tongue over him again before settling in to surround his dick with my mouth and suck on it.

"Ohhh, Johnny!" He gasped as I increased the pressure on him. His body trembled, his cock leaked more pre-cum, and I couldn't take it anymore. I moved swiftly up over his body, spreading my spit on my cock as I did, lining myself up with his arsehole, and claiming his mouth with my own as I slammed my full length into him in one thrust.

He screamed out against my mouth, and I felt him clench around me. I had caught him unawares, but the way his hips moved against mine told me that he was okay and he wanted more.

"Fuck, you feel so damn good around my dick," I told him, smiling down at him, kissing his neck, letting him adjust to taking me so abruptly.

I traced kisses across his collarbone and down to his pecs, wrapping my mouth around his nipple and keeping myself upright with my other hand. I started to thrust into him, deep, hard, and utterly unforgiving.

I adjusted myself. I needed to be sitting between his

legs instead of over him. I wanted his cock in my hand, I wanted to tease him with every thrust of my dick with a stroke of my hand.

He moaned, flexing against me, shifting his hips to get the best from my cock and my hand. Over and over, I thrust hard and deep into him. His hand reached mine around his cock and he squeezed it, encouraging me to be tighter and more forceful around him. I looked at him, and I wanted to say those words. I wanted to tell him what he meant to me, but it felt like it was too soon.

Before I had time to think about it too much, I felt it, that tightening in my bollocks.

"Oh, fuck, Alex. I'm going to come so deep inside you." I wasn't asking him, I was telling him. I knew it was okay, and the thought of him being filled by me without anything covering my cock made my climax that much more powerful. I roared as I felt the first of my cum spurting out deep in his arsehole, needing to pour it all into him, needing to know he was taking everything I had to give him. I gave him one last hard thrust and tug, and he cried out in climax right along with me, hot ribbons of spunk spurting over his belly and chest.

Utterly spent, it took all of my remaining strength not to just collapse on top of him. I slowly pulled out of him and collapsed beside him. He pulled my face to his and kissed me hard, the look on his face speaking volumes without him needing to utter a word.

I pulled him tight against my front and fell asleep with him in my arms.

# CHAPTER 28
## ALEX

When Johnny had first suggested being with him, I have to admit that I thought it wouldn't be for me, that it would be repeating past mistakes of being involved with someone I worked with. But I was wrong. I wanted it. Dear God, I wanted it.

The reality was proving to be very different. Knowing I had been with Johnny had me feeling very liberated. I wasn't sure how that would work out with the band, but it still felt right. Being the drummer with Spitfire Junction was right, and so was being with Johnny.

Johnny caught me in the middle of a daydream as I got myself a drink in the middle of our final sound checks.

"Have fun last night, Alex?" He grinned. I felt the heat in my cheeks. Johnny leaned in closer. "You're mine," he whispered against my ear. "I'll be seeing you later."

"Oh, fuck."

"What are you swearing about?" Travis interrupted.

"I was just telling Alex I have the room next to his." Johnny grinned wickedly.

"Oh, for fuck's sake." Travis rolled his eyes "Can't you

keep it in your pants for five minutes? You're just a walking set of bollocks, I swear."

I winced, and Johnny roared with laughter as Travis walked off, sighing with mock disgust at his friend's libido.

I caught sight of Dexter from the corner of my eye. He'd been handed an envelope by someone from the venue's staff, and when he opened it, the colour drained from his face. Whatever it was, he stuffed it back into the envelope, and when he noticed me watching him, he pulled his mobile from his pocket and disappeared backstage to the manager's office.

"I wonder what that was about," I murmured, more to myself than Johnny.

"I'm sure we'll find out soon enough if we need to."

———

THE SMALL CROWD IN THE GLOBE WAS BUZZING. THE atmosphere was just electric. Dexter got the crowd all worked up for some new material we had been working on. They were singing along by the second time they heard the chorus. It had been a while since I was in a band that had released new material. AP3 had been working on a new album when Preston had pulled his shit and we had broken up our relationship and our band.

The good vibes carried us back to the hotel, where we all went to the bar. Dex's smile had faded, and he told us he was heading for his room.

"You okay, bruv?" Travis asked him.

He nodded. "Yeah, I'm all right." He patted Travis on the back, smiled at me, said goodnight, and waved over to Johnny, who was already at the bar.

I had a drink with the others, celebrated our successes that evening, but I wanted to check on Dexter.

I HEADED UPSTAIRS AND KNOCKED HARD ON DEXTER's door.

"Hey." I beamed at him when the door swung open.

"Hey yourself."

I waited for him to invite me in, but it didn't look like that was happening. Something was clearly troubling Dexter, and I wondered what it could be.

"Uh, can I come in?" I asked to break the silence.

"Oh, shit, yes! Sorry!" He stood back to let me in, snapped out of whatever thoughts he was lost in. "Are you okay?"

"I just wanted to come and tell you thank you for being understanding about me and Johnny," I admitted, more to the floor to him. I couldn't bring myself to look at him. He clearly wasn't happy, and I didn't want to make anything worse.

Dexter looked at me remorsefully. "I'm glad you're both happy, Alex. But I have something you need to hear, and I don't want you to freak out about it, okay?"

I started to panic. "Oh, God. Are you cutting me from the band?" I even sounded panicked. I had practically squeaked out my question.

Dexter shook his head and posted me towards the sofa in his room. "God, no. Nothing like that!"

I moved past him and sat. "Then what is it?" I asked, relaxing a little, looking up to see if I could read his face as to how bad this might be.

"It's about Preston."

*Yip, that was not somewhere I saw this going.* I openly flinched at the mere mention of my ex's name.

"What the fuck can he possibly want now?"

The pity I saw written on Dexter's face made my

stomach knot. I did not want to hear this. He put his hand on my shoulder.

"Dex, you're scaring me."

He moved back to the dresser, lifted an envelope, and brought it to me.

"Apparently, a courier delivered this to the venue today."

I took the envelope from him and pulled out the contents. I recognised the handwriting the second I saw it. Preston's.

*I CAN SEE HOW MUCH YOU ALL ACCEPT ALEX AND CARE ABOUT the band's image. But how much are you willing to do to protect it? I'm betting that once you know what he's like, you'll ditch him faster than your last drummer.*

*I have a tape of him and me, and he's a dirty little bitch, getting fucked in all the ways imaginable.*

*You keep him, I'll release the tape, and you lose the band. You ditch him, and you keep the band.*

*The choice is yours, but I think we both know that he's not worth the trouble.*

MY HANDS STARTED TO SHAKE. A BIZARRE MIX OF ANGER and embarrassment washed over me. I had been eighteen and very stupid. I couldn't believe he kept it, and I couldn't believe he was willing to release it and humiliate us all.

"I'm going to be sick," I told Dexter. The room was spinning.

# CHAPTER 29

## DEXTER

*EARLIER THAT DAY*

I stared at the page in the envelope, trying to take in what was happening, trying to think of how to best handle it, and worried about what it would mean for Alex, or Johnny for that matter, if anything ever came out. I knew only one thing; I had to protect Alex at all costs. I glanced around and saw he had been watching everything I was doing. I shoved the contents back into the envelope and headed to the manager's office.

———

"Eric, I need you to do me a favour."

The voice on the line replied to me.

"That information you've been getting for me, I need it now, like within the next six hours... Yeah, I know that's short notice... I'll take whatever you have so far. From what you've said, it should be enough to know if there's a story there, right?... Yeah, email it to my personal account, mate. Thanks."

Call it a hunch, but I needed to see how many skeletons were in Preston Phillips' closet. When Alex had joined Spitfire Junction, I had called in a favour from a private investigator friend of mine. He'd been looking into our friend Preston very closely. He hadn't told me much over the phone, but he had provided me with enough to know that the fucker had more secrets. Eric had been digging for a while now, and I knew the shit would hit the fan with this dick eventually. Knowing what was going to hit us would lessen the blow eventually, but now he was making threats against Alex, and I wasn't about to take that.

I called Del and told him to come and join me in the office.

———

THE DOOR WAS KNOCKED, AND DELANEY CAME IN.

"Uh," he said when he saw my expression. "What's happened?"

"Preston fucking Phillips is what's happened."

Del's fists clenched tightly at his sides. "What's that wanker done now?"

I sighed. "It's about Alex."

Anger crept over his features. The more I told him, the redder he got.

"He needs to be fucking dealt with," Del seethed.

I agreed with him. The man was worse than a liability, and he needed to be taken care of. "It's in hand," I informed him. "Alex can't know about this yet. No one can. I'll deal with it all after the concert. But I'm going to need a car on standby; I'll be wanting to pay the little prick a visit."

Del nodded. He would make the arrangements for me. I had no idea what I would do to sort this mess out, but I couldn't let anything happen to Alex.

———

THE CONCERT WAS A ROARING SUCCESS. EVEN WITH everything going on behind the scenes, I couldn't help but be caught up in the buzz and thrill that a good gig always filled us with. But when everyone else headed for the bar, I made my excuses with the band and went to my room. I re-read the contents of the envelope as I logged into my email and waited to see what Johnny had sent me.

*To: DEXTER_SPITJUNCT@GMAIL.COM*

*From: eric.mullan@mullaninvestigators.co.uk*

*This guy is a first-class arsehole. I hope you're going to nail his balls to the wall with this.*

*Find attached photos of him with the females in question, dates, ages, birth certificates, etc. There's enough here for a police case, mate. Be warned.*

*CHEERS, ERIC.*

I OPENED THE FIRST PHOTO AND GLANCED AT IT, LOOKING at the names and dates of those in the photo. I clicked next and was greeted by the woman's ID. Fuck. This was huge. More photos had been sent, with evidence of what Eric had been talking about.

*Fuck.*

I jumped when the door to my room knocked. I slammed my laptop closed and headed over to open it.

"Hey." Alex smiled when I opened the door.

"Hey yourself."

He looked at me expectantly for a second. "Uh, can I come in?"

His question jostled me back to reality. "Oh, shit, yes! Sorry!" I said, and stood back to let him come in. "Are you okay?"

Alex nodded. "I just wanted to come and tell you thank you for being understanding about me and Johnny." He was looking down and fidgeting. With everything that was happening today, I pulled him into my arms and held him tight against me. His arms slid around my waist in response and he held me tight right back.

"I'm glad you're both happy, Alex. But I have something that you need to hear, and I don't want you to freak out about it, okay?" I told him.

"Oh, God. Are you cutting me from the band?" he asked, sounding suddenly anxious and vulnerable, and I was reminded that this man had essentially been abused by his ex.

"God, no. Nothing like that!"

I watched his shoulders relax a little.

"Then what is it?" He pulled back from me to look at my face.

"It's about Preston."

He winced at the sound of his name.

"What the fuck can he possibly want now?"

I nodded towards the sofa. "I think you should sit down."

"Dex, you're scaring me."

His backside hit the sofa, and I sighed. He was there to share his happiness with me, and there I was, about to put fear into him and tell him something that might pull his life apart.

"Apparently, a courier delivered this to the venue today," I explained, and handed Alex the envelope. I waited and watched him while he opened it and digested the contents.

The envelope and note started to shake, and I watched his chest rise and fall rapidly. "I'm going to be sick."

"He really has one, then?"

He nodded, his face pure white. "I'm so sorry." A tear escaped from his eye and ran down his cheek.

*Oh, Christ.* Instantly, I was in his space. "Hey. No, no, no. This isn't on you!" I put my arm around his shoulder. "We will sort this, together, all of us," I told him. "We're not about to let anything happen to you while we have breath left in our bodies, Alex."

"How the hell do I fight this?"

"*We* will." I pulled my phone from my pocket and called Johnny. "My room, mate. Now, and bring Travis." I hung up.

Within minutes, there was a knock on my door.

"What the fuck?" Johnny was pissed. Travis looked past him and caught a glimpse of Alex.

"What the fuck did you do?" he growled at me.

Alex got up. "No! It wasn't Dexter. Look." He held out the note from Preston.

Both men stepped into the room. Travis took the note from him and Johnny read it over his shoulder.

"I'm going to fucking kill him," Travis fumed.

"You can wait in the fucking queue," Johnny snarled.

Alex touched them both tenderly on the chest. "Stop," he pleaded. Johnny and Travis swarmed around him and held him against them, forming a protective cocoon around him.

"I've told Alex that we will deal with this together, and that we will protect him and make sure it's okay," I told them as I moved in to join their cocoon. Johnny and Travis let go of Alex on one side and let me surround him with them. We stood there for a few moments, Alex in the middle of our Spitfire Junction burrito.

"Thank you." He sighed, looking at each of us in turn. "I'm so sorry I brought all this to your door. What the hell do I do?"

We'd let our arms drop, and he moved out from the middle. Travis was thinking. Scheming, in fact; I could tell.

"I have an idea that *we* can do," he piped up, emphasising the 'we' to make sure Alex knew he wasn't in this alone.

"Let's hear it," Johnny said. "And it better have me smacking him in the teeth at some point."

Alex smirked.

Travis looked at me. "Mate, I know you, so I'm going to assume you've been talking to your friend again. But my idea is, whatever he's found, we use it and blackmail the dirty little bastard right back. Play him at his own game."

I nodded. He knew me too well.

"You've been spying on him?" Alex asked.

I shrugged. "I wouldn't call it spying."

Johnny raised an eyebrow.

"Well... not really. More... protecting the band's image. When you joined us, Alex, I had my friend do a little digging to see if there was anything about Preston that might come back to bite us in the arse. I'm glad I did, because now we can look out for you better than I could have hoped."

"Oh, fuck. I'm not going to like this, am I?" Alex asked.

I shook my head. "Probably not." I looked at Johnny and Travis, knowing they could read me well enough to know that shit was about to get serious, and Alex was about to be hurt. Again.

Travis took him by the hand and got him to sit back down on the sofa again. "We're ready," he said, and Johnny sat on the other side of them and took Alex's other hand.

"Preston is a cheater." I held up a finger to pause Alex in his reply. "A serial cheater. Steph wasn't the only one. But there's an unfortunate pattern that has emerged. Remember the age you were when you first got with him? That's his thing. He likes them younger. But, ah... "

"Sick cunt," Johnny interrupted.

"How young?" Alex asked.

"The youngest Johnny has found so far is fourteen years old."

Alex got up and started pacing the room.

"Alex," Travis pleaded.

Alex shook his head at him. "No, Travis." His eyes went to Johnny, who was about to stand. "Don't."

"Alex."

He stopped and looked at me. "I don't care what you have to do. Deal with him. If you need to push me out of the band to save yourselves, do it. I can't deal with anything more from him." He turned and headed for the door. Johnny went to move and catch him.

"John," I said, and shook my head when he looked at me. He stopped, and all three of us watched as Alex left the room and the door closed behind him.

# CHAPTER 30

## DEXTER

Travis had a pretty reasonable idea, to be honest. Blackmailing the blackmailer. It was risky, but I really couldn't think of anything else that would work. We all agreed that the biggest thing we needed to do was protect Alex. We knew that might cost us the band, but with everything that was going on between Johnny and Alex, and how injured Preston had left him, we also agreed that he was more important.

Johnny and I were going to see Preston, and Travis was going to stay with Alex. Del had the car waiting for us, and I knew from Johnny where Preston was.

"Are you ready for this?"

Johnny nodded.

"Then let's get the fuck out of here," I told him, putting the postcode Johnny had supplied into the satnav and heading away from the hotel.

———

It was two hours later when we finally arrived in Reading, where Preston was hiding in a riverside apartment.

"You're sure this is the place?"

I looked at my phone, then at the building in front of us. "That's where the investigator says he is."

Johnny nodded. "Let's get this fucking over with then." He headed for the main doors of the swanky apartment block.

The security guard greeted us at the door. I got myself ready for having to blag my way into the building.

"Oh my God, Spitfire Junction!"

Johnny grinned at me. "Alright, mate?" He smiled at the guy, holding out his hand for him to shake.

"Johnny Scott, fucking hell. What are you guys doing here?"

"We just needed to call in and see Preston Phillips," I told him, hoping he would welcome us on up. The guy's face fell, and I thought he was going to refuse us entry.

"Oh, that prick." He snorted. "That tosser is up in apartment 4D. He's been strutting around here like he owns the joint."

Johnny nodded. "Yeah, he's a bit of a wanker, isn't he?"

The guard agreed. "Not being funny, but that Alex Hart seems like a lovely fella, and what he did to him is just fucked up."

I grinned and patted him on the back. "You hit the nail on the head there, mate. We're just off to have a little chat with him. Thanks, fella." I strode off and left Johnny to shake the guy's hand one more time.

———

Johnny pounded his fist against the door and then stood to the side, out of Preston's immediate line of sight.

"What the fuck?" Preston grumbled as he opened the door and came face to face with me. Johnny stepped in between me and Preston with a face like thunder and slammed the door back wide, forcing the arsehole to take a step back so we could get into the flat.

"What the fuck indeed, ballbag." Johnny growled. "Someone's been a very naughty boy."

"John!" I tried to get my friend to rein in his anger.

The second Johnny started to keep his cool, Preston got back in his face. "Yeah, you fucking gorilla. Back in your box."

"Phillips, if you like your face how it is right now, I suggest you try shutting the fuck up and listening for a change."

I walked right past him, sat down on the sofa, and crossed my legs, waiting for them both to join me.

"What the fuck do you want, Lovell?"

"I came to talk to you about your lovely little note. I mean, I'm honoured that you went to all that effort, but unfortunately, we're going to have to decline both of your kind offers."

Johnny smirked.

Preston seethed. "Oh, I think you're going to have to pick one, and since I really can't see why anyone would pick my used cast-offs over the fame and hot ass that being in *Spitfire Junction* brings, it's going to have to be that you send poor little Alex on his merry way."

There was something about the way he said the name of the band that made me want to let Johnny lay into him. But it wasn't the time for that just yet.

I glared at him. "The best thing you ever did was letting that man go."

Johnny smirked and leaned in, keeping his voice low. "He's so far out of your league. He's top of the premiership, and you're bottom of the third division."

"I can have top-class platinum pussy and ass. Why the fuck would you think Alex Hart is above *me*?" Preston scoffed.

I moved into Preston's space and watched the expression on his face flash a little fear. "Because, Prickton... I can call you Prickton, right? Because, *Preston*, you, my friend, are the lowest piece of shit scum I have ever had the misfortune of breathing the same air as." I sat back and waited for his next move.

Preston stood. He needed to give himself back what he thought was the superior position. He put his hand in his pocket, and for a split second, my heart stopped, worrying about what he would pull out. It was a USB memory stick.

"This will just have to find its way into the hands of *The Sun* then, won't it?" He smirked.

Johnny looked at me, and I knew exactly what he was thinking. He was going to smack some manners and sense into Preston and take the memory stick.

*Soon.*

"So, lads, as fun as this little chat is, do we have your final decision? My sloppy seconds, or the band that you've been working so hard to preserve the image of?"

Johnny's hands were balled into tight fists. He was ready to pounce, and I was about to let him.

"Anything else to add to that nice little rant, Prickton?"

"I always knew Alex was a bit of a rock star slut, but I never realised just how desperate he was. I mean, he dropped me for you," he spat, looking Johnny up and down.

Johnny boiled over, and I didn't say a word. He stood

and moved towards Preston, his face full of fury, and I thought Preston was about to piss his pants.

# CHAPTER 31

## JOHNNY

That was it. I just couldn't take it anymore. Listening to this fucking prick talking such trash about my man was a fatal mistake. It was in that moment that I realised I had actually fallen for our drummer. I honestly would have committed murder for him right there and then.

"Alex's little finger has more self-respect in it than your entire body." I grabbed him and pushed him hard against the wall.

"Hit a raw nerve, did I, big guy?" He smirked at me. "Honestly, I didn't think blonde bimbos with muscles were really his thing."

I glanced over at Dex. "Reminds me of a line from a cheesy eighties film," I told him, and then looked back to Preston, getting right in his face. "Your ego is writing cheques that your body can't cash."

Dexter spluttered out a laugh.

Preston glared at me. "Fancy yourself as a Maverick?"

I leaned in closer. "Iceman, and you're about to find out why."

"Oh, I can see the headlines now," he gloated. "Alex's sex tape scandal and Spitfire Junction's assault charges and time in prison."

I was done. I just couldn't listen to him any longer. I pulled back my right fist a fraction, and while he was laughing about the fate he thought he was going to bring down on us, I punched him square in the guts.

He crumpled down the wall like a sack of shit. "I'm going to have you done," he wheezed, badly winded.

Dexter nodded towards the sofa, and I picked up Preston by the scruff of his neck and planted him back on the sofa.

"Let me explain to you how this is going to go down, *mate*," Dexter started, sitting on the footstool in front of Phillips. "You see, I have this friend who I like to have look into things for me from time to time, and he found out something very interesting about you."

Preston's eyes widened. Ha! We had the bastard.

"Ohh, yes. You see, Preston, we know about the four-teen-year-old boy from your last tour. We know about the fifteen-year-old in Milton Keynes who had an abortion and how you paid for all of it, and we also know that you now pay her family £2000 a month."

Dexter looked up at me. "What do you think, Johnny? Does it seem like our new best friend is hiding something?"

I grinned. "Sounds fucking like it."

"Doesn't it just." He turned back to Preston on the chair. "Only, I know exactly what you've been hiding, you slimy cunt. You have a thing for young boys and girls. You fucked one, and oops, you got her pregnant. But you couldn't have that now, could you, Preston? Evidence of what you do, and a tie to one person for the rest of your life. So, you paid for her abortion, and you pay for her silence. But, if I can find that out, then I'm pretty sure the police might be able to find out just a little bit more, huh?"

"So, here's what's going to happen. You're going to give me that USB stick. You're going to promise that any other copies are destroyed, and as long as that happens, the police never need to find out about your little indiscretions. Do you agree?"

Preston nodded.

"You'd better, because if you don't, it'll be the boys in blue knocking at your door next time, not us," I warned him.

Preston handed over the memory stick. I took it from him and put it in my pocket.

"You're scum, Phillips. If you ever come near Alex again, I will personally break your fucking legs. Are we clear?" I asked.

"Fine," he mumbled.

"Then I think we're done here." I nodded to Dexter, and we headed for the door.

# CHAPTER 32
## ALEX

I FELT LIKE I WAS CLIMBING THE WALLS. TRAVIS KEPT trying to calm me, trying to get me to sit down or to talk about something else. But I couldn't. All I could think about was Preston. *What would he do? What would he say? What if he disagreed? What if he made them pick walking away from me? What if they pushed me out of the band?*

Every single thought was spinning around in my head, and no matter how hard I tried, I just couldn't get rid of them.

"Alex, everything is going to be fine, I promise you," Travis said, catching my arm as I stalked past him for what felt like the millionth time.

"But you don't know that!"

He shook his head. "Alex, I know those two would never let anything happen to you. We decided that unanimously. We protect *you* above everything else."

"What?" I squeaked.

"We picked you. Fuck the band. Fuck fame. Fuck it all. It's all about protecting you."

I stopped and stared at him. "Oh my God. Why? Why would you do that? I'm not worth that!"

He pulled me down to sit beside him and held my hand. "Are you fucking kidding me?" He held me close against him. "Alex, *you* are important, as our drummer for Spitfire Junction, and as the man who made Johnathan Scott grow a heart. You have made big changes to our brother, and that makes you important to us. You are *always* going to be worth it as far as we're concerned."

I shook my head, and Travis grabbed my shoulder and jostled me until I looked at him. "You are important to us, especially Johnny. You belong with Spitfire Junction, Alex."

I felt tears well up in my eyes. No one had ever made me feel as wanted as these men had in the last few months. I had always been not enough. I had always been scared someone would realise that all the things Preston had been pouring into my head over all these years were right and see me as the fucked up, worth nothing mess he made me believe I was.

"Oh, Alex." He hugged me. "Don't cry. You're amazing, and we love you." I stiffened at his words, but he continued to squeeze me and put me completely at ease. I sighed against him and tried not to think about Preston Phillips and everything that was happening while Dexter and Johnny were away.

————

I GUESS AT SOME POINT IN THE EVENING, I MUST HAVE fallen asleep. I woke to find myself in bed. I put my hand out behind me and came across a rock hard warm abdomen. An arm slipped around me and pulled me tight against him.

"Are you okay?"

"Johnny?" I turned over to lie on my back and look at him. His arm remained across my stomach. "What happened?" I wasn't sure I would like the answer, but I knew I had to ask anyway.

"I'm all good, gorgeous. Everything's been taken care of."

My mind churned with twenty million questions, all bursting to be asked.

"What did he do?"

Johnny pulled me against him and kissed the tip of my nose. "Shhh."

"Johnathan!" I said, shoving him. "This is important! What happened with Preston?"

He opened his eyes and looked at me. "He won't be releasing anything. We took his memory stick, and he says he'll be deleting all other copies. I told him I knew about what he'd done. I told him that if anything ever happened to you in any way, I would take it straight to the police. I'm not entirely convinced I shouldn't be doing that anyway."

"You mean it's really over? I'm not being kicked out of the band, and he's not leaking any sex tapes anywhere? It's all okay and I'm staying where I am?"

Johnny pulled me tighter against him. "I'm very happy for you to stay exactly where you are, Alex."

"Did you hit him?"

Johnny smirked. "Maybe."

"In the face?"

"Are you worried I'll have marred his pretty features?" He laughed in the darkness.

"Fuck, no. I'm worried he'll have bruises for the press to ask him about next time he's in public."

Johnny's hand idly traced over my stomach in lazy circles. "My fist was aimed squarely at Phillips' guts. It's not a bruise he will be able to easily show off."

I thought about it for a moment. "Good. As long as your fist is okay."

"Like a fist, do you?"

I elbowed Johnny lightly in the ribs. "Ha bloody ha."

He laughed at me, and I settled beside him, staring at what I could make out of him in the darkness.

"How come you're in bed beside me?" I thought out loud.

"Because I wanted to be here when you woke up. I wanted to be able to kiss you and tell you that everything was going to be okay."

Dammit, what was it with this man and making me feel the heat in my cheeks?

"You're sexy when you blush," he added.

"How can you tell that in the dark?"

"I don't need to see you to know what makes you blush, baby."

I blushed even more.

"Is that what you want? To sleep with me, I mean."

I could just make out his lips curling in the darkness. "I would love to sleep if someone would stop talking."

"Oh."

"Goodnight, Alex," he said, and moments later, a soft snore drifted across to me.

# CHAPTER 33

## JOHNNY

HE WAS STILL FAST ASLEEP BESIDE ME WHEN I OPENED MY eyes the next morning. He was on his side, facing away from me, his back spooned in against my front. I lay there, enjoying how good it felt to have him pressed against me.

The morning wood I was sporting wasn't exactly helping the situation, though. Not when I had a warm, sexy body pressed up against me. I slid my arm around him again and pulled him tight against me, my cock lining up perfectly against his ass, making me want to groan.

I lay there, with nothing else to do but wait, because I wasn't about to attempt to take advantage of a sleeping man. He sighed and wriggled back against me even more. His arse fitted against me perfectly, and the throbbing in my cock was driving me insane.

I spread my hand out over his stomach and gently pressed myself against him. His body responded, and he let out a soft moan.

"You're not asleep, are you?" I whispered.

His hand covered mine, and he rolled his hips back against my dick.

"Nope." He laughed softly.

"Dammit, Alex. You've been driving me insane for ages."

He laughed again. "Like I could sleep with *that* poking me in the ass."

I thrust my hips against his arse. "You mean *this*?" I was rewarded with a second soft sigh. "Damn, your noises are sexy," I said and nuzzled against his neck, my lips connecting with his bare skin.

"Mmm, Johnny," he murmured.

I slid my hand over his skin as I nibbled on his neck. His nipple pebbled instantly at my touch, and my cock twitched against his arse.

Fuck, I needed to be inside him. He turned the upper part of his body towards me, and I took that as an invitation to claim his mouth. I lifted my head and kissed him hard, showing him everything I had been feeling for him for weeks. I wanted to be with him. He was never allowed to leave the band, but I would rather have the band fall to dust than ever lose him. My tongue ran along his lips, and he parted them to let me inside his gorgeous mouth. I had never been with a man like him; he was amazing. I couldn't believe I was lucky enough to be in bed with him; to touch him, to kiss him, and soon, to make love to him all over again.

Alex turned his body to mine, kissing me back hard. He ran his fingers over my chest and played with the hair he found there. I grabbed his ass, and he lifted his leg over my hip in response. God bless the universe. He was naked, and nothing was keeping me from what I wanted.

His hand slid down my torso and headed right for the band of my boxers. He put his palm over my cock and slid it over my length.

"Fuck!" I moaned, feeling the electricity his fingertips

generated in my skin. When he wrapped his hand around my dick and started to stroke me up and down, I kissed him hard and pulled him against me.

I was so turned on by a man who clearly knew exactly what he wanted and wasn't afraid to take it. And as long as he wanted to take it from me, I was more than willing to let him do exactly that.

His firm grip was driving me crazy. I needed more, but before I could say anything, he was pushing me onto my back and had straddled me. I watched in delight as he lay over me, pressed his delicious body against mine, and captured my mouth.

I couldn't keep my hands to myself. I ran them all over him, touching his back and grabbing his ass. He said nothing, but he was showing me just how much he wanted me. I could see how damn hard he was for me, and I couldn't wait to find out what it would be like to get deep inside him while he was on top.

He shifted and lifted his pelvis off mine. His hands went to my boxers. He freed my throbbing dick and held it in his hand. With his other hand, he spat in it and rubbed it over my cock. Then he positioned himself over my dick.

I watched in awe as Alex seated himself on my dick, and it slid deep inside him in one slow, torturous move. He moaned out as he took me all the way in, and the head of my prick deep within him.

I ran my hands up his thighs, stroking him teasingly before I let them come to rest on his hips, helping him move up and down on my length.

"Jesus, Alex." I hissed as he slammed himself down on me again. He smirked at me, and a gentle roll of his hips had his head falling back and a long sigh spilling from him. He was a goddamn vision.

He put his hands on my chest and moved himself up

and down on me. He let his hands roam over my skin when he was setting himself back down again. It felt amazing. He felt amazing.

With one hand I grabbed at his ass and hips as she moved on my dick, with the other, I firmly held on to his cock. I watched him avidly as his body flexed and moved, bringing himself to the edge of satisfaction on top of my body. Every inch of him was a delight to behold. When he caught my gaze, my heart fluttered in my chest, and my balls tightened.

I rolled my thumb over the tip of his cock. Alex's voice got louder, and the delicious sounds he made just made me want to pound into him harder. I needed to come, and I wanted it to be deep inside him. I knew it was a stupid idea, but it was him, and how he made me feel. I wanted to be with him. I couldn't imagine feeling like this for anyone else, and being able to dump a load deep in his arse seemed like the perfect expression of exactly that.

With one hand holding onto his hip, and the other gripping him firmly while letting my thumb make circles around that sensitive tip, I drove my cock deep and hard into him as much as I could.

"Oh, fuck, John. You're so fucking deep."

That was me a goner. The sound of my name on his lips as he moaned was all it took. I would have promised him anything in that moment. My heart was his, as I was. I kept up the pace with my hand, grabbed his arse, and pounded into him until he came. Greedily, I came right along with him, holding him on me as I filled him with cum.

He flopped forward to kiss me, and I held him in my arms, not wanting the moment between us to be over, knowing only too well that soon we would have to get up and face the day.

# CHAPTER 34

## JOHNNY

ONCE MY MAN WAS SATED, I SHOWERED AND HEADED OUT to pound the streets for a while. On the way back from my morning run, I had called into the local Sainsbury's for my favourite smoothie, only to have a gutter press headline catch my eye.

*Fuck.* It was a story about Del's daughter and Preston Phillips. He'd knocked her up and then demanded that she have an abortion. I scanned over the story on the front page.

### *PRESTON PHILLIPS IN UNDERAGE BABY MOMMA SCANDAL*

*Preston Phillips (37), was unavailable for comment today, as the scandal of his numerous liaisons with young girls was uncovered. Not only was it discovered that he had impregnated the daughter of his ex-manager, Delaney Joseph, (54), but an insider claims that when confronted with the news, Spencer demanded that she 'get rid of it.' After further investigation, the Daily News can report that she isn't the only 'baby momma' Phillips has made such demands of. Several other women, varying in age from 15 to 24 have come forward with similar stories. The police are said to be making enquiries.*

I COULDN'T READ ANY MORE OF IT, BUT KNOWING THE BOYS would be very interested in this new development, I scooped up a copy of the paper and bought it along with my beverage.

———

I WENT TO MY ROOM, HAD A SHOWER, AND HEADED BACK down to breakfast to meet everyone else, the paper tucked under my arm. I sat and waited for the right time to share my discovery.

"Ready to hit Bristol?" Travis asked as he bit into his slice of toast.

"I'm looking forward to this one," Alex chimed in. "I haven't been there in years!"

"What the hell took you to Bristol?" Dexter laughed.

"I had a friend in the University of West England, and he took me to Pop, Bubble, Rock in Lanes. That's where our gig is, right?"

Dexter laughed and shook his head.

"Sure is, Alex," I confirmed.

"Is your hand okay?" He was genuinely concerned for me.

I grinned at his sympathy for me and nodded, showing him the lack of damage.

Dexter looked at Alex. "Have you decided what you're going to do with the information we have?"

He shook his head.

"I think it has to be Alex's decision," Travis added.

I pulled the paper out from under my arm. "About

that..." I put the newspaper down on the table where everyone could see it. "I spotted this when I was out for a run earlier."

Alex took the paper from the table and studied the front cover. Not for the first time where Preston Phillips was concerned, I watched the colour drain from his face.

"It's gone public?" His voice was low, and Dexter took the paper from him, scanning the front page.

"Damn." He passed the *Daily News* over to Travis for him to view the cover.

"Wow, I didn't think it would get out like that." He looked at Alex. "Sorry, Alex."

He swallowed and looked around absently. "I, uh, I feel sick. I think I'm going to head up to my room until we need to go, okay?" He wasn't really asking us, but he looked like a lost little child, asking permission.

Johnny looked at him with compassion and touched his hand gently. He pulled his hand away like it had burned him. "I just... I can't." Without saying another word or making eye contact with any of us, he got up and left the table.

I patted Johnny on the shoulder. "Don't take it personally, mate. It's not you."

He shrugged. "I know. It's just..."

"It kills to not be able to fix it for him," Travis finished.

"I hear ya, guys. I hear ya," I agreed, my eyes falling on the doorway he left through.

# CHAPTER 35

## ALEX

Preston Phillips was turning into the nightmare that never ended. It wasn't enough that he was a cheater. It wasn't enough that he had claimed my virginity when I was seventeen. It wasn't enough that he had broken my heart and ruined our band. No, Preston *had* to have a scandal attached to him. A seedy, disgusting scandal, and no doubt, now I would be sucked into it.

I'm not sure what good I thought it would do, but I lifted my laptop and went straight to Google. I put in *Preston Phillips* and hit 'Search'.

My stomach flipped when the 'Top Stories' section was filled with images of young women and men snapped trying to get away from the press, with headlines about what he had done, what he had said, and the ages they were when they were with him.

Suddenly, I felt too warm, and the room felt too closed in. I needed to escape. I needed to be anywhere but where I was. I grabbed my phone, my room key card, and I headed for the lobby and front door.

I hit the pavement outside and just started to walk. I

didn't know where I was heading, I just needed to get away. Away from Preston. Away from Del. Away from Spitfire Junction.

About fifty minutes later, I found myself at the Waterfront Park. I found somewhere to sit and just stared out at the water.

I was barely there for five minutes and my phone started to ring. 'Unknown Number' flashed on the screen, and without thinking, I answered.

"Is that Alex Hart? Mr Hart, it's Derek Newton here from the *News of the Day*. Is it true that Preston Phillips has been arrested?"

"What?"

"Preston Phillips has been arrested. Did you know? Do you care to comment?"

"No." I hung up the call before they asked anything else.

*What the hell. Preston had been arrested?* I didn't think my stomach could twist up any further. I knew that, given everything I had been up to in the last week in particular, it shouldn't really have bothered me what happened to Preston, but there was something about it that just seemed to leave me feeling sullied.

The man I had loved, who I had had my heart broken by, had changed the entire dynamic of our relationship into something sinister. This wasn't the man I had loved and lost my virginity to. This was a predator, and my virginity had been a trophy. It wasn't love; it probably never had been on his part. It was me being a pawn in the game he liked to play. A sick and twisted game where there really were no winners. Just damaged little girls and boys and a creepy bastard.

I didn't get any more time to dwell on it when my phone rang again. I pressed the green button to answer.

"Mr Hart, this is Bernard Lewis from the *National Inquirer.* Have you any comment to make on the arrest of your former lover, Preston Phillips?"

I didn't even bother to answer them this time. I just hung up. Again, the phone rang. I hit reject. And again. And again. And again.

I lifted my hand and was about to walk to the railing and throw my phone into the sea when I noticed the name on the screen.

'Johnny Scott calling...'

I didn't say anything when I picked up.

"Alex, are you all right? Where are you? We're all worried sick!"

"Have you seen it?" My voice was low. I was broken.

"Seen what? He didn't release that video, did he?" Johnny sounded angry when he mentioned the video.

"No. He's been arrested."

Johnny covered the mouthpiece, but I could still make out his voice faintly. *He says he's been arrested. Google that shit, will you, Dex?* "Where are you?"

I wasn't all that sure other than at the waterside. "I don't know."

"Alex, you're scaring me." I could hear the stress in Johnny's voice. I should have felt guilty that he was worried about me, but all I felt was numb.

"I've got to go." I didn't wait for his reply, I just ended the call.

# CHAPTER 36
## JOHNNY

He sounded so lost that my heart broke the second I heard him. He didn't tell me where he was, but I had to find him and make it all okay for him.

"He's not okay, is he?" Travis looked pained.

"Nope." I shook my head.

Dexter tapped on his laptop, and then turned the screen to us.

Preston Phillips arrested on sexual offence charges, including indecent assault of a female under sixteen and buggery of a male under sixteen.

"Jesus Christ." Travis gasped as he read the selection of headlines.

Dexter nodded. "And this is the man Alex lost his virginity to. I can't imagine how fucked up that must feel."

"I need to find him," I stated, tapping on my phone, remembering that we had all started to share our locations with each other the last time Preston showed up and I took a cut to my face in Sheffield.

There he was, a little blue dot moving along the water-front. "Dexter, find out everything you can about this arrest. Travis, get on the phone to Patrick and find out what he can do legally to keep Alex as far out of all this shit as he can. I'm going to go get my man."

Patrick was our lawyer; he handled anything we needed. Travis and Dexter agreed with my plan, not that I stuck around long enough for them to voice any real complaint. I was out the door and heading for the lobby as fast as my legs could get me down the fire stairs.

Once out on the street, I managed to grab a taxi right at the door of the hotel that had just been dropping off another fare. "Listen, mate, I'll give you ten times your fare if you can get me to the Waterfront Park as quickly as you can!"

———

My little lost boy was just sitting there, staring at the water. His phone rang as I approached, and I watched as he pulled it from his pocket, looked at the screen, and launched it into the water in front of him.

"You threw your phone in the water," I said, announcing my presence.

"Vultures just keep calling." He continued to stare at the point where his phone had disappeared.

I stepped into his space and pulled him tight against me, wrapping my arms around him. I waited and felt the tell-tale vibrations in his body that told me he was sobbing. I kissed the top of his head gently and just waited.

"I feel so disgusting," he mumbled into my chest in a voice so low I almost didn't hear him.

"You are the least disgusting man I've ever met. In fact, I think you're the most amazing man I've ever met." He looked up at me, and time stopped. In that instant, it was just him and me, and no one else in the whole world existed.

"I wish I felt amazing," he said, without looking up.

"You feel it to me." I squeezed him that little bit tighter. "I understand how you're feeling, more than you know, but you can't let it define you. You can't have it be everything you are."

"You had your virginity taken by a man who turned out to be a paedophile?"

Nice. Sarcasm.

"No. My mother's gay best friend when I was fifteen."

Confused eyes looked up at me.

"My mother was an eternal drunk. One of her usual bar bunny mates came on to me, totally shit-faced. I was young, stupid, and just learning the fun I could have with my dick. I thought I was such a stud. What I really was, was a child who was used and taken advantage of."

He tucked his head in against my chest again and squeezed me tight in return.

"Let's get you back to the hotel." I kissed the top of his head again and held his hand as I walked him back to the waiting taxi.

# CHAPTER 37

## ALEX

THE GUYS TRIED TO TALK TO ME, BUT I WAS NUMB. I JUST couldn't take it all in. The first man I had ever loved was the stuff of nightmares. He had used me when I was too young to know any better, and while I had been building a life with him, he had been cheating on me. *Was it cheating if those involved were too young to consent?* He was making young girls pregnant. He was fucking young boys. I just felt sick.

Patrick did his best for me. He tried to keep me out of it as much as he could. We had a few injunctions granted, so some of what the press wanted to put out never made it to print. But it was hard, and it was vile, and I just couldn't deal with it.

Music was the only thing that saved me; the only thing keeping me holding on. I felt guilty. Guilty that I was pushing the guys away after how wonderfully they had welcomed me into their Spitfire Junction family. Guilty that I didn't see what Preston was really like and stop him. Guilty that I was this silly little naïve boy who believed every lie he ever told me. But once on stage, I played my heart out. I poured all of my emotion into the tracks and kept the tiniest sliver of my sanity that way.

I had been seventeen when Preston and I got together, and while that didn't make me one of his victims, the fact that I was a virgin seemed to play directly into the darker side of his character. I spoke to the police at length about it all; my age, my virgin status, the finer details of his behaviour towards me, did I notice this and that. They offered me counselling for abuse victims, and I think that was when it really hit home. That last semblance of sanity I had been holding onto just melted into nothing.

I felt sick. I felt as though all those years with Preston had been one big hideous lie, a joke that I was only now finding out I was the punchline of.

I gave my virginity to a man who had a thing for underage partners, and who revelled in taking their virginities. I wasn't special to Preston Phillips; I was just another trophy he had needed to claim.

The last nine years of my life were obliterated in mere days as more and more information came out about Preston's involvement with underage partners.

The press hounded us mercilessly in every town we stopped at for a gig. Every time I left the hotel, they were on me like a pack of wild dogs, looking for some snippet of bitterness, some token soundbite, or a photo of me in tears or looking like I was locked away crying over Preston and this whole sorry mess.

I did cry, though. Away from the cameras, and journalists, and prying eyes. Johnny happened to knock on my door at just the right time.

*"Sweetheart." His voice soothed me, and he wrapped his thick arms around me.*

*"I'm sorry."*

*"Shhh!"*

*I couldn't quieten though; all these thoughts were rolling around and around in my head.*

*"You don't need to keep torturing yourself with this. He's really not worth it," he reassured me, and as much as I knew he was right, I just couldn't get my brain to disengage.*

*"It's like I've been told I'm just someone's fetish-fulfilling wet dream."*

*Johnny's chest rumbled.*

*"Don't you dare!" I scolded, looking up at him. My gaze was met with playful, cheeky eyes. I couldn't help it. A laugh bubbled out of me too. I shook my head at him and blew my nose with the hanky he offered.*

*He kissed my cheek. "That's my guy." He smiled.*

*"Is your mind ever out of the gutter?"*

*He grinned. "You said 'wet dream'. You know I've the mental age of a schoolboy for things like that."*

*"Child." I snorted.*

*"Sweetheart," he retaliated, and pulled me tight against him, his mouth capturing mine as he did.*

NEXT TIME, IT WAS TRAVIS WHO HAD TO DEAL WITH MY overwrought emotions. He collected me from the police station where I was answering their questions for a second time.

*"SEAT BELT."*

*"I know." I sniffed.*

*"Want to talk?"*

*I looked at him and thought about it for a moment. "No. No, actually I want to get angry."*

*Travis glanced at me from the driver's seat before pulling out into traffic. "Okay. Let's do something about that." He turned the car sharply in a U-turn and headed in the opposite direction.*

*"Where are we going?"*

*Travis smiled. "You need to burn off some of that anger."*

Fifteen minutes later, we were outside an old, converted warehouse.

*"What's this?"*

*Travis took the keys from the ignition and opened his door to get out. "Come and find out."*

*I got out of the car and followed him into the large sprawl of building. The space had been subdivided with a main atrium full of skylights, and plants, and sofas down the middle. Travis took my hand and led me to the big double doors at the very end of the space.*

*T's Boxing Gym.*

*"T's?" I looked at him, puzzled. "Do you know T?"*

*He nodded. "I do, and so do you. You're looking at him. T - Travis."*

*"This is yours?" I was shocked. Travis hadn't once mentioned having a business away from the band.*

*He greeted a few of the staff by name and led me to the punch bags in the corner.*

*He handed me gloves and helped me lace them up. He placed his hands on my hips and showed me the best stance. He held the bag still. "Picture Preston's face."*

*I hit the bag, and it swayed against Travis.*

*"I thought you hated him?"*

*"I do!"*

*Travis braced himself against the bag. "Then show me."*

*Again, I pulled back my right fist. This time, before I launched it at the bag, I thought about my anger at finding him cheating. I thought about how hurt I felt to have the good memories of the last nine years smashed to smithereens because of everything I had found out. Next time, I swung my right fist forwards into the punchbag; my left quickly followed. I started pummelling the bag, noticing Travis stumble with my first punch, but then sturdy himself for the rest of my barrage of anger.*

*A*N HOUR LATER, MY ARMS AND HANDS ACHED, BUT *I* FELT SO *much better than I had when all this mess first came out.*

*"Arms hurt?"*

*I nodded. Travis took my right arm in his hands and skilfully manipulated the muscles, repeated it on the left arm, and then moved behind me to start into my shoulders. As soon as his thumbs hit my neck, I let out a soft groan.*

*"Feel good?"*

*I nodded, the ability to form words having left me. He grabbed my arms and shook them out, and in that instant, I felt so much better than I had in a while.*

*"Let's go back to the hotel before Johnny comes to hunt me down," he whispered against my ear.*

*I laughed and nodded.*

I WAS SO GRATEFUL FOR EVERYTHING THE GUYS WERE doing, but there was still a dark cloud over me I just couldn't shift, and I wasn't sure what could be done to ever change that.

# CHAPTER 38

## DEXTER

Alex decided that the information we had on Preston should be passed to the police. It was no longer a weapon; it was evidence that could lead to a stronger conviction. He was pretty much screwed regardless. One of the girls he got pregnant lied. She didn't have an abortion, she had a son. DNA had confirmed that he was Preston's, and her age at the time of the boy's birthday, confirmed by her birth certificate and his, proved that Preston had been with underage girls. She had been one of them. His future was pretty bleak. He was going to prison, and not for a short spell, either. He'd never be bothering her or anyone else again.

None of that gave Alex any real comfort. He was heartbroken, and the nature of the heartbreak just made it harder for him to pick himself up again. He had the occasional moments of peace, helped along by gestures from Johnny, Travis, and me, but for the most part, he was just a little boy lost.

The last few weeks of the tour flew by, and while Alex played his heart out and smiled, and did everything else that made him a great bandmate, his spark was gone. His passion for life. Hell, even his cheek was gone, as was the sarcasm. I couldn't stand seeing him like that. I understood why. I knew he was down; I knew he blamed himself on so many levels, but he was just as much Preston's victim as the others were. Something had to change.

Our last gig was coming up that night, and I decided we needed to make it special for him. I called the guys and discussed it with both of them. We all agreed. Everything was set.

———

THE END OF THE FINAL GIG ARRIVED, AND I HELD MY HANDS up to silence the crowd.

"Guys, we have a big announcement for you all."

A huge cheer echoed around the venue.

Travis went over to Alex and pulled him out from behind the drum set. Johnny went off stage to grab a present for him. He was escorted over beside me, front and centre stage.

"You all know the amazing Alex Hart, right, guys?"

Another huge cheer erupted.

"He's done an amazing job this tour, right?"

The crowd cheered and shouted 'yes'.

"Well, I just wanted to let you know that Alex will be staying with us, with Spitfire Junction, permanently, as our new drummer."

He blinked at me in complete shock. Johnny appeared beside him with a big bottle of Champagne and gave him a huge kiss on the cheek. The crowd cheered more. They clearly agreed with Alex being finally announced as the official replacement for Andy.

"You're part of Spitfire Junction," Travis told him, and grinned.

"Alex! Alex! Alex!" the crowd chanted.

I could see the tears filling his eyes as he took everything in.

"We love you. Right, guys?" I asked the crowd. The largest cheer I think we have ever had at one of our concerts echoed around the stadium.

He smiled a warm and genuine smile, and a tear escaped and rolled over his cheek. He took the mic from my hand and looked out at the audience.

"Thank you all so much. The last few weeks have been hard for me, and you guys have seen me through it all," he said, looking at us as he said it.

I smiled back at him and nodded. Johnny blew him a kiss, and Travis smiled back at him too. Something on Alex's face had changed; something had lifted from him. He was coming back to us.

As the crowd cheered, we all linked arms and walked off the stage as a foursome.

# CHAPTER 39
## JOHNNY

Something definitely changed in Alex when Dexter announced him as the permanent replacement for Andy. He looked like a person whose life was suddenly that little bit lighter. He wasn't back to the Alex who'd walked into the audition that day, but he was back to being close to that. I knew time would have him feeling better; distance from the event would help endlessly.

Since getting back from the tour, the guys and I had been talking about getting some properties where we could all live. We had been talking about it for some time and nothing ever came about it, but now we wanted to make Alex feel good, so it had to be a place he would be interested in too. We just hadn't told him that part yet. We had been looking in and around the Surrey area, trying to find the perfect place.

Travis came bouncing into the studio with his tablet in his hand. "This is it!" He handed it to me, and I looked at the screen.

"Four luxury apartments in a converted country estate.

We could all have our own space, but there are communal areas for things like a gym, a home studio, a pool, stables, and a massive garage." I flicked through the photos. "Damn, that's a fucking nice piece of land."

Dexter took the tablet from me and had a look too. "I agree. Want to arrange a viewing?"

Travis nodded, took the tablet back, and started looking up the details for the estate agent. Alex came in just as he was finishing up his call. He looked at him and raised an eyebrow. I knew what it meant. *Do you think we should take Alex?* I nodded slightly back at him.

Dexter got there before us. "Alex, Travis's just sorted a viewing on an amazing house in the Surrey Hills. Want to come and look at it with us?"

He was surprised but agreed.

---

WE HAD WORKED WELL INTO THE EVENING ON THE START of some new material for a new album now Alex was 'official', even though we had all known he would be staying with us regardless. I was tired as fuck when the guys arrived at my place to take us to the viewing.

"Alright, you lovely bastards." I laughed. "Let's get to Surrey!" I sat beside Alex and we set off for the hour and a half trip into the Surrey countryside.

A while into the journey, my curiosity was getting the better of me. "So, Alex. What do you look for in a house?"

Dexter looked at me in the rearview mirror and smirked.

He thought about it before he replied. "Storage, a great garden, room to move around, and I guess the right company in it from time to time."

I grinned. Travis's choice ticked all Alex's boxes without even trying. This was going to be great. We chatted about houses, about how the album was going, and our general plans for the future.

When we arrived at the house, we realised the photographs online really hadn't done it justice. It was beyond amazing.

"Oh, wow!" Alex gasped, summing up pretty much perfectly what the rest of us were thinking. As we made our way up the gravel driveway, we spotted the estate agent waiting for us right outside.

"Nice find, Travis. This is fucking amazing," I congratulated him as I admired the outside of this incredible house.

"Can't lie, mate, I'm impressed myself now I'm here." Travis laughed.

"Come on," Dexter added. "Let's go look inside."

We got out of our car and went to shake hands with the estate agent and see just what the estate had to offer.

———

WE VIEWED ALL FOUR APARTMENTS, EVERY ONE OF THEM with four bedrooms, including a massive master bedroom with an en-suite that included a tub and a lot of space. We walked around the massive expanse of the property and the grounds and countless 'wows' and gasps were uttered. And then the guy showing us around left us to our own devices.

"So, if you could have any apartment, which one would you pick?"

Alex grabbed me by the hand and led me to the one he would choose. "This one!" he said as we stood in the doorway. He walked into the bedroom there and started to explain all the things he would have set up and where. He showed me where he would put his bed and explained why. He stood by the window, gazing out at the massive garden, and I moved in behind him.

"I like where you would put the bed, but I'm a little worried the neighbours might see me naked when I'm in here with you." I grinned and kissed his neck. He was about to protest something, but my lips nipping at his skin halted him. He melted back against me, and my hands instinctively went to his waist, pulling him back against me. His body moulded to mine and my hand roamed up towards his cock.

"Damn, you really can't keep your hands to yourself," Travis said, announcing his presence.

I held Alex pressed against me and lifted my head from his neck. "Nope." I grinned.

I put my lips back on his neck and shoulder and rubbed my hard cock against him, letting him know just how I felt about Travis knowing we were together. He squirmed in my grasp, the heat radiating from his cheeks as he tried to get free.

I heard Dexter's voice behind me. "Guys, are you.... what the fuck?"

Alex pushed me away, and I laughed.

Dexter grinned. "Could we at least sign a contract on this place before you're shagging in the bedrooms?" He laughed, and Alex went the brightest shade of crimson I'd seen on him yet.

"Oh my God." He was embarrassed as hell and broke past Dexter in a power walk. I looked at Travis and we both just grinned and shrugged.

"You are a pair of horndogs," Dexter scolded.

Travis looked at me and shook his head. "I guess this means you're official now, does it?"

"Maybe." I burst out laughing and walked past him, looking for Alex.

"The agent's in the foyer," Dexter called after me.

# CHAPTER 40

## ALEX

I COULD FEEL THE FIRE OF LUST AND HUMILIATION SCALDING my face as I moved through the house to get as far from the apartment and the guys as I could. It was almost as though Dexter coming into the room snapped me back to my senses and made me realise what I was doing.

I wanted Johnny. I wasn't ashamed of what we were doing, but it just felt in that moment like I had been caught out doing something naughty, like a child, and that I needed to get away from it and how much I wanted him. I knew I wouldn't be able to run away from it forever, but just for now, for a few minutes, I needed to.

I walked into the foyer and found the estate agent. "What do you think of the property?" he asked, and I welcomed the distraction from my previous antics.

"It is just amazing. It's a gorgeous house, it really is. And the way the apartments have been worked into it, it's just incredible."

"Do you think you would like to take the estate?" he asked.

I was about to explain that I was just there to look, and

that I wouldn't be signing on the dotted line, when Johnny came into the room behind me.

"What do you say, Alex? Do we get the house?"

I blushed and nodded. "I can see you guys here."

"But can you see *you* here?" Travis asked as he walked into the foyer.

Dexter wasn't far behind him. "You can see yourself in that apartment, can't you?"

Johnny looked at my face and read my emotions instantly. "We're asking you to move in with us, Alex. We want to have you here too."

I nodded.

"Is that a yes you'll move in with us?" Travis asked.

"Yes," I agreed. "But only if I get that apartment."

Dexter grinned and threw his arms in the air.

Travis smiled at the estate agent. "How soon can we get the keys?"

"And can we get the option to buy the place after a year?" Dex added.

The agent handed over all the paperwork, a rental agreement for a year, alarm details, and all the relevant information. Johnny, Dexter, Travis, and I took turns to sign the contract. Dexter made a call to Patrick and made sure a year's worth of rent was paid in full to the rental company.

The house was ours. The agent handed over the keys, made arrangements to drop us the spares, and left us to enjoy the house.

Johnny pulled me back against him as Dexter and Travis walked to the door with the estate agent, thanking him for his time. He crushed his lips against mine and kissed me hard.

"I'm so glad you've agreed to stay with us," he breathed against my lips.

My body melted against his as usual, and Dexter and Travis returned.

"Dammit, Johnny. We turn our backs for two minutes." Dexter laughed to announce that they were back in the room with us. Johnny's smile made him part his lips from mine. He looked at Dexter and shrugged, stepping back and raising his hand as though he was surrendering.

Dexter laughed and looked at me intensely. "So, you're really going to live with us, with *him* here?" he asked. I nodded, and he laughed. "Christ, Alex. I hope you know what you're getting into with the walking testicle."

I glanced over my shoulder at the man who had stolen my heart. "Oh, I think I'll cope."

Damn, things were definitely going to get interesting.

"Well, fuck," I heard Johnny say as I let out a laugh. "I can't believe I'm moving in with a man. What's the world coming to?"

Dexter smirked. "Oh, he'll be fine. He's getting an apartment of his own that he doesn't actually have to share with you."

Johnny looked fake injured by Dexter's comment and we all walked out of the front main door of what was, apparently, now all ours.

# CHAPTER 41
## ALEX

THE AIR IN THE CAR ALL THE WAY BACK TO MY HOUSE HAD been electric. They tried to divert the conversation to other things, but there was a raw excitement about us all living together.

"What will you do with your house?" Travis asked as we arrived outside it.

"I'll probably rent it out. I mean, I own it." I didn't want it to seem like I was keeping it as a back-up plan, a 'just in case'. I just didn't think it was smart to sell a property I owned outright. Besides, I had inherited it, and I would never want to be parted from it. "It was my gran's," I explained. I looked at the floor, feeling like I was disappointing them somehow.

Travis smiled. "So, you'll be like me with the gyms. A little sideline. An investment in the future." Relief washed over me. He understood.

Johnny squeezed my hand. "I'm still looking for my sideline."

"I'm not sure professional sperm donor is a thing." Dexter laughed. I snorted. Travis coughed.

"Fuck you," Johnny retorted. "I know plenty of women who would pay good money to get their hands on my baby batter."

I felt jealousy wash over me; I couldn't help it. We hadn't talked longevity. We hadn't talked children, but the thought of Johnny having a baby with anyone else made me suddenly feel possessive and angry.

Dexter was looking at me in the rear-view mirror. "John, I don't think your *baby batter* is going anywhere." He nodded in my direction.

Johnny kissed my hand. "Don't worry. All my sperm is just for you now, and you can have it for free."

Travis roared with laughter beside me before getting out of the car. Dexter was snorting too. "Bellend." He chuckled as he got out of the car.

"Unbelievable." I snickered in shock at his comment and followed Travis out of the car. Johnny shrugged and got out, following the rest of us to my front door.

I put the key into the lock and paused for a second. The heat of the guys behind me reminded me that my friends were about to be in my house. The thought that the last man to be in my house like this was Preston flashed through my mind. Dismissing it, I turned the key and let Johnny, Travis, and Dexter follow me in.

————

Dexter had a bottle of Champagne with him to celebrate the fact that we were all moving in together. Johnny ordered a Chinese takeaway. Travis sorted us a film to watch on Netflix. We all sat in my living room, enjoying each other's company, enjoying the food, and enjoying the wine.

Dexter held up his glass. "To new beginnings and moving forward."

"Cheers." We all toasted.

As the evening went on, I found us all gelling well. I was on the sofa with my head on Johnny's shoulder. His fingers had begun to lazily trace circles on my knee. It was a feeling that sizzled all the way up my leg and reached my cock. I started to fidget against him. I looked up at him. His green eyes sparkled with lust and he shuffled in the seat just enough that I could see his cock hard against his jeans. *Fuck.*

"Enough of this shit. Bedroom?" he asked, cocking his head towards the hallway.

Travis and Dexter laughed. "I think that's the end of the night for us." Dexter laughed. "Come on, mate. Let's go get a taxi." He pulled himself out of the chair he was in and he and Travis left without another word.

"You're so rude!" I scolded Johnny. He threw me over his shoulder and stormed upstairs, ignoring me.

"Which door?" he demanded.

"Second on the right."

He pushed the door open and set me on the edge of my bed. He stood looking at me. I wanted him, but now I had him in front of me in my own bedroom in my own house, I wasn't sure where to start.

I needn't have worried. Johnny made the first move. He fell to his knees between my legs and kissed me passionately. He licked along my lips, silently demanding I let his tongue dance with mine.

I relaxed, giving into the moment and kissing him back, wrapping my arms around his neck. He pulled me against him, his hands grabbing my arse and forcing my wet sex to feel the outline of his erection through our clothes.

*Damn.* I was wearing too much. He was wearing too much. I needed to be naked with him. I pulled at his t-shirt and he took the hint, pulling it off over his head.

Johnny stood and stepped back, unfastening the fly on his jeans. Once they were discarded on the floor, he moved into the space between my legs and pulled my top over my head. He looked like he was about to devour me. My hands went to his waistband.

"I want to taste you." I reached into his boxers and freed his cock. I looked up at him as I guided the head of his dick towards my mouth, licking the pre-cum from the tip.

He hissed as my tongue circled him. I stared at him as I slid my mouth down over his hard length.

"Jesus, Alex." He fisted his hand in my hair and moved me a little farther down on his cock with every thrust.

"Alex. I need you on the bed."

He moaned and pulled his cock from my mouth with a pop.

"Stand up," he demanded. He undid my jeans, pushed them to the floor, and I stepped out of them. He kissed me softly on the neck and pulled my t-shirt off over my head. "Get on your hands and knees facing the headboard." Johnny patted the bed, and I followed his instructions.

I felt the bed dip behind me and moaned as Johnny ran a finger along the crack of my arse. I felt his saliva dribble over my arsehole, and he worked his fingers into me, teasing me with a slow finger fuck. I moaned again, begging him for more.

Johnny started pressing on that little area right inside me with his fingers, and I couldn't help myself. I was going to come. I felt my orgasm build in my lower stomach.

Glancing at Johnny was enough to send me over the edge. The lust on his face was just the most delicious sight

I'd ever seen, and I cried out, my arse pulsing around his fingers, and a small amount of milky fluid dripped from my cock.

"Oh, fuck." I gasped as he worked his thumb over my bellend again, coating his digit with my milk before licking it off. I couldn't wait any longer. "Oh, God. Give me your dick!" I begged.

The gorgeous man behind me didn't need any more invitation than that. Johnny slipped his cock between my ass cheeks and slid into my ready arse.

My body was overloading with feelings; every nerve was on fire. His strong hands caressed me, grabbed me, held onto me. I felt loved and adored. I was showing *my* man how I felt about him, and he was doing the same with me.

Johnny's movements were slow and deep. Calculated to drive me suitably insane, and they were.

The noises I was making around Johnny's cock increased.

"Hmmm, fuck!" Johnny moaned. "You're so fucking tight."

Oh, God. I was close again. Feeling another orgasm building as his cock rubbed against my p-spot, I surrendered to all the sensations.

I came apart loudly on Johnny's dick, moaning out, sending vibrations through him, causing him to come with me as he flooded my hole with his delicious spunk.

"Fuck, yes!" Johnny grabbed my hips tight and slammed deep into me one last time.

My legs and arms turned to jelly, and no longer able to support myself, I collapsed on the bed.

Johnny collapsed too and moved me so he could spoon in behind me. We lay there, spent, on my bed.

"You okay?" he asked.

"Mmmm," I replied.

"Can't talk yet?" Johnny laughed.

"Mmmm."

He leaned in and kissed my forehead. "I love you, Alex."

"I love you too," I croaked, overwhelmed with the emotion and sensations of the evening.

His hands were still on my body. I was loved, cherished, and utterly exhausted. Sleep claimed us both. The next day, we would move in together. My world had changed infinitely since I met Johnny, Dexter, and Travis, and joined Spitfire Junction. I was more contented than I had ever been in my life. This was where I belonged. I was with a man who loved me completely. Tomorrow would be the start of forever, I could feel it, and wherever it led and whatever it brought us, we would face it all together, as a band, and as a couple.

# EPILOGUE
## ALEX

## *THREE YEARS LATER*

We sat at our table, waiting. Everything we had worked on over the last three years was brought to fruition in that moment. We waited, we held our breath, and then it happened, again, and again, and again.

"And the Brit Award for British Album of the Year goes to… Spitfire Junction for *Closure*."

"The Brit Award for British Single of the Year goes to… Spitfire Junction for *Breathing Fire*."

"The Brit Award for British Rock Act goes to… Spitfire Junction."

"The Brit Award for British Live Act goes to… I can't believe it, guys. This is definitely your night. Spitfire Junction!"

"The Brit Award for Global Success goes to… Holy cow! Spitfire Junction!"

We had done it. By the time we got on to the stage to accept our fifth and final award, the guys and I were deliriously happy. They pushed me forward to the podium.

"Oh, right, my turn, huh?"

The crowd laughed.

"I know these guys have thanked everyone before this, but, ah, I would just like to offer my thanks to them. Travis, Dexter, Johnny, thank you from the bottom of my heart. You took a chance on a lad with a stormy background and you have supported me, and loved me, and I couldn't ask for better friends to surround myself with. WE DID IT!"

The crowd went crazy, and we floated back to our table on the biggest buzz we had ever had.

———

THE EVENING WAS INCREDIBLE, AND WE PARTIED 'TIL THE small hours of the morning. Travis came over and pulled me tight against him so I could hear him. "Dexter wants to know if you're going to the label's after-party?"

Johnny smirked, and I glared at him. "I can't. I have to get back to the sitter and let her go home!"

Travis chuckled. "You do what you've gotta do. We're all heading over."

I smiled and hugged him. This had been the night that we had worked on for so long, and it was finally paying off. Dexter waved over to me as he took Cassie's hand with a grin that warmed my heart. I was glad to see him finally so happy; Cassie was a lovely girl, and he really deserved her. Now, if I could just get my other friend hooked up, I would be a very happy man.

"I'll take you home, you loon." Johnny laughed and pulled me against him on the opposite side to Travis. I bumped my hip into his to get space between us again.

"Ass."

He laughed again. I hugged Travis and asked him to make sure Dexter was okay.

"I'll make sure he gets home, don't worry. I'm not drinking any more tonight. I want to remember every damn detail."

I hugged him tight, and when I let go, the crowd at the party quickly swallowed him up as he moved back through them. I turned to Johnny, and he was still grinning.

"Come on then, Cinderella. Let's go and let the *baby*sitter go home."

———

AN HOUR AND A HALF LATER, OUR LIMO PULLED INTO THE driveway of the estate. A year after we rented it, we had asked the owner if they would be willing to sell and we took it on as ours; *all* of ours. Together.

After three years together, Johnny and I had moved into my apartment together. Dexter had the idea of starting a record label, and Johnny's apartment had been the perfect place to house it all. As for Johnny and me, we were still as in love and lust as we were when we started. An addition to our family just seemed like the next logical step.

"Daddy's home!" I called out when I walked in through the front door to our apartment. I listened to the footfall thundering towards me and waited for that lovable face to appear. "There he is!"

Alfie sprinted over to me, and I knelt down to his level and opened my arms wide.

Alfie practically dived on me and knocked me on my ass. I wrapped my arms around him and kissed the top of his head over and over. Kate, our sitter, appeared around the doorway.

"Hey, guys. Good night?"

Johnny grinned at me and Alfie and nodded to Kate. "We won them all. Five fucking awards!"

"That is fantastic!" She smiled.

"Has my boy been good?" I asked her.

She smiled at him fondly. "Good as gold. And no chewing on your drumsticks this time."

I held Alfie's face and kissed him again. "You're such a good boy! Who's Daddy's boy?"

Johnny told Kate that the car was still outside and that she could use it to head on home, and he closed the door behind her. He turned and looked at me again. "You treat that puppy like a damn baby." He laughed.

"He *is* my baby."

Johnny snorted. "Yeah, a seventy-five pound, six-month-old, Great Dane baby." And with that, he walked towards the kitchen, made a clicking sound, and Alfie took off, trotting behind him.

"Yeah, he's Daddy Johnny's baby too." I laughed, following my favourite men to the kitchen.

Johnny pulled me towards him as I filled Alfie's bowl with water. "So, I think we have time to do a little celebrating."

I set the bowl on the floor, and I turned to Johnny, wrapping my arms around his neck. "Sounds like a plan to me." I leaned into him and crushed my lips to his. Johnny's hands lifted me under the arms and held me up to his height. I wrapped my legs around him and held on tight to him. I could feel his hard cock pressed against my own. "Take me to bed," I breathed against his lips.

"Don't need to tell me twice."

I clutched him tighter as he headed upstairs to my bedroom. I grinned as Alfie followed us.

Life was going to get very interesting for us, and I

couldn't wait to share it with the man I loved, and the men who gave me the chance I needed to flourish. Whatever happened in the future, Spitfire Junction was so much more than a band now. We were a family.

# ALSO BY DREW DUNCAN

*Just Because Series*

Because I Need You

Because I Want Him

Because I Didn't Know

Because It's Always You (Coming late 2021)

*Serenade Series*

Hart Beats

Love Notes - Coming 2023

Title TBC - Coming 2023

Keep up to date with the latest release - Join Drew's mailing list

# ABOUT THE AUTHOR

Drew is an Irish author with a panache for sarcasm and a love of the random, her cynicism knows no bounds, but she's a secret hopeless romantic who likes to let her characters sizzle on the pages.

She lives her with two children, and dreams of escaping to Hampshire, the home of Jane Austen. When she's not writing, you can find her knitting, crocheting, shouting at Ireland playing rugby, and of course reading.

———

Keep up to date with all the latest releases and info from Drew by joining their mailing list here:
www.drewduncanbooks.co.uk/newsletter

———

facebook.com/authordrewduncan

instagram.com/authordrewduncan

tiktok.com/@drewduncanauthor